# Disney Learning

## Wonderful World of

# SPACE

Written by Andrew Fraknoi

For Nikki:
With cosmic good wishes
*[signature]*

# Parents' Note

How hot is the Sun? Do black holes really exist? Is there life on other planets?

Disney's *Wonderful World of Space* has been created to answer these and so many other questions, allowing your child to learn about the universe in a fun and meaningful way. Formatted in a simple question-and-answer style, this book has been designed to appeal to a child's limitless curiosity about our amazing universe.

Simply organized, each chapter profiles a different aspect of astronomy, with questions accompanied by lively answers written by an expert astronomer. Stunning full-color photographs and illustrations and favorite Disney characters accompany fascinating facts to help make the learning come to life.

Disney's *Wonderful World of Space* has been designed as a learning tool that is certain to educate children, while inspiring in them a lifelong interest in what exists beyond our planet's atmosphere.

## About the Author

Andrew Fraknoi teaches astronomy to more than 800 students a year at Foothill College in the San Francisco Bay area. He also works for the Astronomical Society of the Pacific, an organization founded in 1889 to help astronomers explain the universe to the public. Part of his job is directing Family ASTRO, a project to create astronomy games and kits for families. He is coauthor of a college text-book on astronomy and has edited two books of astronomy and science fiction. He also appears regularly on local and national radio shows, explaining astronomy ideas in everyday language. The International Astronomical Union has named asteroid 4859 Asteroid Fraknoi to honor his work in expanding the public understanding of astronomy.

He would like to thank his son, Alex, who is 13, for making excellent (and funny) suggestions for improving the book and for all his support during the writing and editing of it.

For information address Disney Press, 114 Fifth Avenue, New York, New York 10011-5690.
Visit www.disneybooks.com

Printed in Singapore

ISBN-13: 978-0-7868-4969-7
ISBN-10: 0-7868-4969-X

Library of Congress Cataloging-in-Publication Data on file.

First Edition
1 2 3 4 5 6 7 8 9 10

Written by Andrew Fraknoi
Vetted by Stephanie Parello
Cover design and interior art direction by Alex Eiserloh
Book interior designed by Q2A Media
Disney character art © Disney Enterprises, Inc.
Pixar character art © Disney Enterprises, Inc./Pixar
Slinky® Dog © James Industries
All rights reserved.

# Contents

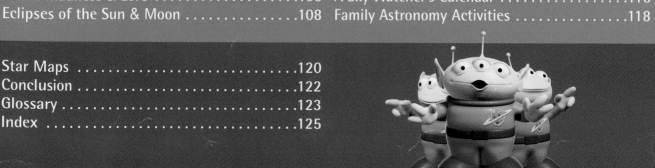

# Our Fascination with Astronomy

Have you dreamed about what it would be like to walk in the red deserts of Mars or to visit the rings of Saturn? Did you ever look at the stars on a clear night and wonder if any of them also have planets orbiting around them? Do you wonder, "Are there other beings like us out there?"

Welcome to the wonderful world of space. People have been fascinated by the sky and the universe for as long as they have walked the Earth. But in the last 50 years we have discovered more about what's out there than in all the time that came before. We've found beautiful new worlds, mind-boggling distances, and awesome explosions that have shaped our world.

## What Is Astronomy?

Astronomy is the study of everything beyond Earth—from our nearest neighbor, the Moon, to the farthest reaches of space. Astronomy, like all sciences, is constantly being updated as new discoveries are made. Answers to old questions give rise to new questions. If you watch the nightly news or read magazines and newspapers, you'll hear about a new discovery in astronomy several times a year. This book will help you understand what all the excitement is about.

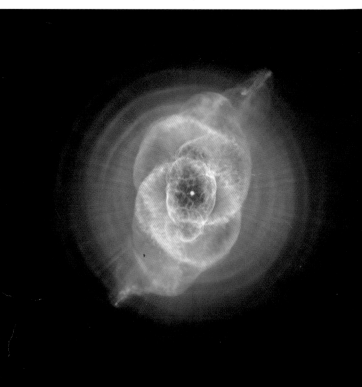

*People have always been fascinated by stars. Big telescopes reveal more of them than our eyes alone can see.*

*New technology allows astronomers to see amazing things in deep space, such as this dying star.*

## The Realms of the Universe

Astronomers usually divide the world of space into three different realms, or parts. First, our local "neighborhood" in space is called the solar system. It is made up of the Sun and its family. The solar system includes one star (the Sun), eight planets, several dwarf planets, more than 160 moons, and lots of smaller chunks of rock and ice. Although it seems big to us, the solar system is only a tiny part of everything that's out there.

Compared to other planets in our solar system, Earth (third from left) is tiny.

The second realm astronomers talk about is our galaxy. Our Sun is one of billions of stars in a giant disc-shaped island of stars called the Milky Way Galaxy. Our galaxy is so big that it would take a traveler 100,000 years to go from one side to the other—that is, if they could travel at the speed of light! Besides stars, our galaxy has lots of gas and dust— raw materials from which new stars, new planets, and maybe even new organisms are being made all the time. But the Milky Way Galaxy is not alone. There are billions and billions of other galaxies—other islands of stars with billions of stars in them, too.

The last and biggest realm is the universe. It is everything that we can ever learn about—all matter, space, and time. The universe is made up of many groups of galaxies, stretching out

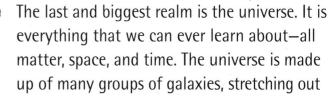

The Andromeda galaxy is one of the Milky Way's closest big neighbors.

in all directions. Like explorers mapping a new continent, we are just beginning to understand the arrangement of all those groups of galaxies and how far they extend.

Astronomy, like every science, is always a "progress report"; scientists learn more and more each time they do new experiments. This book is a progress report, too; it tells you what we have learned so far. But it also mentions some of the mysteries we hope to explore in the future.

As shown in this painting, astronomers have begun to discover planets around other stars in our galaxy.

## Astronomy Is Always "Old News"

One of the most amazing things about astronomy is that when we look at the stars, we see them as they were long ago, not as they are today. Here's why: the reason we know what the stars are doing is that they send a lot of light out into space. Some of their light eventually reaches Earth. Although light is the fastest messenger in the universe, it still takes some time to reach us.

The light we see tonight from Alpha Centauri, the star closest to the Sun, left the star 4⅓ years ago. It took 4⅓ years for the light to make its way through all the space between the star and us. Because the distance is so great, astronomers measure it in light-years, the distance light travels in a year. So, Alpha Centauri is said to be 4⅓ light-years from Earth. Sirius, the brightest star in the sky, is eight light-years away. That means its light left the star about eight years ago.

So, the news—or views—we get of Sirius is eight years old. But because stars change very slowly, the news from eight years ago is still current. Other stars are hundreds of light-years away, and their news is even older.

The biggest galaxy near to the Milky Way is more than two million light-years away. This means the light we see tonight left that galaxy two million years ago! You might think that it would be frustrating for astronomers to get such delayed news from the universe. But it's not. As astronomers look farther and farther out into space, they are looking farther and farther back in time. This way, they learn about the history of the universe—and follow the clues back to the beginning.

## Astronomy In Action

Reading about the stars and planets is great, but nothing beats looking at the sky on a clear, dark night. You can stretch your mind by thinking about stars as faraway suns. They seem small only because they are very far away. In addition to stars, maybe you'll see a little slice of the Moon, a shooting star, or a satellite moving slowly overhead. Depending on your position and the season, you may see other planets, too. To get even better views of

*Even beginning sky watchers can spot a shooting star.*

the night sky, borrow binoculars or a telescope, and head far out of town—to a place where artificial lights do not lessen the blackness of night. If possible, visit a planetarium, a theater in which the stars are projected onto a dome.

## How to Use This Book

Flip through the pages to get a glimpse of what's to come. Check out the Table of Contents and make a mental note of the things you're especially interested in learning. From there, it's probably a good idea to read each chapter from start to finish, since some of the information earlier in each chapter will help you understand things that are discussed later on. You'll notice that most of the ideas are expressed in a question-and-answer format. This is because one of the best ways to learn something new is to ask lots of questions. At the end of the book, you will find a glossary, with explanations of many special astronomy words that might be new to you. There is also a list of Web sites that can help you further explore the universe.

When you've read through this book, we think you'll agree that space really is a wonderful place. And with many types of new telescopes and space probes being planned and launched, exploring it is only going to get more exciting in the future.

## How Fast Are You Moving When You Are Sitting Still?

Relax for a minute and sit down in a comfortable chair. How fast are you moving right now? You might think that's a weird question since you are sitting still. But you are only sitting still as measured by Earth standards. If you could see yourself from outer space, you'd see that "sitting still" isn't really possible. That's because you're moving with Earth as it zooms through space. How fast are you going? Well, here are some facts:

- Earth spins on its axis at about 1,000 miles per hour (1,600 km/h) when measured at the equator. If you're in the United States, you're spinning with Earth at about 700–800 mph.

- Earth orbits the Sun at 67,000 mph (108,000 km/h). You, of course, are along for the ride!

- The Sun and our entire solar system swirl around the center of the Milky Way at almost 500,000 mph (800,000 km/h). Hold on! You're traveling right along with it.

Why aren't you dizzy? You don't feel any of these motions because gravity holds us firmly to Earth. And space is mostly empty, so there is no friction. So the next time you think that you're just sitting still and doing nothing, think again!

# Planets & Moons

Our Solar System

Sizes not to scale

Venus

Earth

Mars

Jupiter

How many planets are there? When your parents and teachers went to school, they learned about the nine planets in our solar system. To sky watchers today, the answer is not so simple. Even astronomers have trouble agreeing on how many planets there are! Recently astronomers decided that there are only eight major planets that orbit, or go around, our Sun: Mercury, Venus, Earth, Mars, Jupiter, Saturn, Uranus, and Neptune. Pluto and several worlds that are smaller than the other planets are now called dwarf planets.

Starting in 2006, astronomers organized the solar system into four categories. Planets are worlds that go around the Sun, are large and round, and have orbits that are clear of other planets. Dwarf planets are smaller and have orbits that can sometimes cross each other. Moons are worlds that orbit a planet. Small Solar System Bodies, such as asteroids and comets, also orbit the Sun but are so small they never become round.

Every planet in our solar system is different. Planets can be rocky, like Mars, or large balls of liquid and gas, like Saturn. They can be hot, like Venus, or freezing cold, like Neptune. However, they all orbit the Sun. The time it takes to make one complete trip around the Sun is the planet's year. Every planet also turns on its axis, an imaginary line that runs through its poles. The time it takes for a planet to turn once on its axis is called the planet's day.

In addition to the planets, our solar system includes 160 or so moons. Moons vary greatly. Several are bigger than the smallest planet, while many others are just rocks a few miles across. Even moons that orbit the same planet can be amazingly different from one another.

As scientists build better telescopes, they continue to find more worlds in our solar system. In the future, maybe you will be one of those making the discoveries!

▲ Jupiter's moon Europa

▲ Comet NEAT

# Mercury:
## The Heavy-Metal Planet

Mercury is the smallest **planet** and the world that is closest to the Sun. It has no **atmosphere**—layers of air—around it. Because Mercury is so close to the Sun, the sunlit, daytime side is broiling, with a midday temperature of 800°F (425°C). With no air to hold the heat in, the night side of Mercury gets freezing cold, plummeting to -280°F (-175°C). So Mercury is not a place that people will be visiting anytime soon.

Mercury's surface is pockmarked with craters, evidence of rocks and other debris colliding with it over billions of years.

## What is Mercury made of?

Most of the **core**, or inside, of Mercury is made up of heavy materials, especially metals such as iron. The rocky outer layer, or **crust**, is just a thin skin covering the heavy-metal core. One possible reason that Mercury is made up mostly of its core material is that long ago, when the planets were first forming, Mercury was hit by small worlds flying around the **solar system**. They tore away much of its lighter outside layer, leaving mostly the heavy inside behind. Because of continued bombardment by space rocks, what's left of its surface is covered with big, round holes called **craters**.

*I NEED A PLACE WITH SOME ATMOSPHERE!*

## FAR-OUT FACTS:

**Size:** 3,000 miles across (4,800 km)

**Daytime Temperature:** 800°F (425°C)

**Nighttime Temperature:** -280°F (-175°C)

**Length of a Year:** 88 Earth days

**Length of a Day:** 59 Earth days

**Distance from Sun:** 35 million miles (56 million km)

**Fun Fact:** Mercury has the largest difference in day and night temperatures of any planet—over 1,000 degrees Fahrenheit.

## Why does Mercury have so many craters?

All planets have been hit with space debris over time, but on Mercury, these assaults leave nearly permanent impressions. Whenever chunks of rock fall from space onto a planet's surface, they explode and blow out a bowl-shaped basin that's much bigger than the size of the rock. But not having an atmosphere makes a big difference for Mercury. More rocks hit it, because, unlike a planet with a heavy atmosphere, such as Earth, the smaller rocks do not burn up before reaching the surface. Also, not having an atmosphere means that there is no weather to wear the craters down over time. So on Mercury, we can see thousands of big and small craters made over billions of years. The biggest crater, called Caloris, is 840 miles (1,350 km) wide. That's greater than the distance between New York and Chicago. Such big craters on Mercury are full of smaller craters made by later impacts.

## What's in a Name?

Mercury is named for the messenger of the gods in Roman mythology. A messenger has to be fast, and Mercury is the fastest-moving planet, whizzing around the Sun at a speed of 105,000 miles per hour (170,000 km/h).

*This painting shows the* Messenger *spacecraft orbiting Mercury.*

## How are Mercury's craters named?

The crater Caloris was named for a Latin word that means "hot." It was given this name because it's located at the hottest spot on the planet. Astronomers decided to name all the other large craters on Mercury after artists, writers, and composers of music. So you can find craters named Bach, Shakespeare, and van Gogh on the planet. You can also find the craters Sholom Aleichem, named after a Yiddish writer; Saikaku, named after a Japanese poet; Echegaray, named after a Spanish playwright; and Bartok, named after a Hungarian composer. As you can see, the crater names are taken from many different cultures.

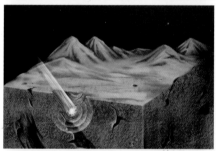

## Have any spacecraft explored Mercury?

Only one spacecraft has visited Mercury so far. In 1974 and 1975, *Mariner 10* flew by the little planet three times, giving us terrific black-and-white pictures. In 2008, NASA's *Messenger* spacecraft will fly by Mercury and eventually go into orbit around it. Scientists expect to get amazing photos of the planet's surface.

## Why is a day so long on Mercury?

Every planet's **day** is based on the time it takes to **rotate** once on its **axis.** Mercury rotates very slowly, taking 59 Earth days to spin just once. But the little planet takes only 88 Earth days **revolve** around the Sun. This means that its day is two thirds the length of its **year**!

*Even a small rock can leave a huge crater on a planet's surface.*

# Venus:
## Too Hot to Handle!

Venus is often called Earth's "sister planet" because it is nearly the same size as Earth and is made of the same materials. But the family resemblance really ends there. Venus has a thick atmosphere, but it doesn't have air that we could breathe. And the planet is hot, hot, *hot*, with a typical day and night temperature of over 850°F (450°C)—making it hotter than any other planet. Venus is also a cloudy world, where there has not been a single clear day for billions of years.

## Why is Venus so much hotter than Earth?

The reason is something scientists call the **greenhouse effect**. In a greenhouse on Earth, sunlight passes through special glass, building up heat inside, which cannot escape. The thick atmosphere of Venus acts like a giant greenhouse, keeping the planet much hotter than it would be otherwise. This thick air blanket has kept the heat building up on Venus for billions of years.

## What is Venus made of?

Venus, like Earth, is made of rocks and metals. Its crust is made of rock, but the planet is much too hot to have oceans or lakes or any liquid water on it. Venus has many volcanoes, which sometimes flood the surface with molten lava.

## Could humans live on Venus?

Any confused tourists who try to land on Venus without lots of protection would have several choices of how to die. They could be broiled by the high temperature. They could choke to death on the air, 96% of which is carbon dioxide, which is too high a concentration for humans to breathe. They could be crushed by the air pressure, which is so great it feels like being more than half a mile underwater on Earth. Even if they survived all that, they would soon die of thirst, since Venus is drier than any Earth desert.

▽ *On this false-color radar globe of Venus, the tallest areas are brown, the middle-height areas are green, and the lowest areas are blue.*

## FAR-OUT FACTS:

**Size:** 7,500 miles across (12,000 km)

**Temperature:** 850°F (450°C)—hotter than any other planet

**Length of a Year:** 225 Earth days

**Length of a Day:** 243 Earth days. Venus has the longest day of any planet.

**Distance from Sun:** 67 million miles (108 million km)

**Fun Fact:** Venus spins *backward* on its axis.

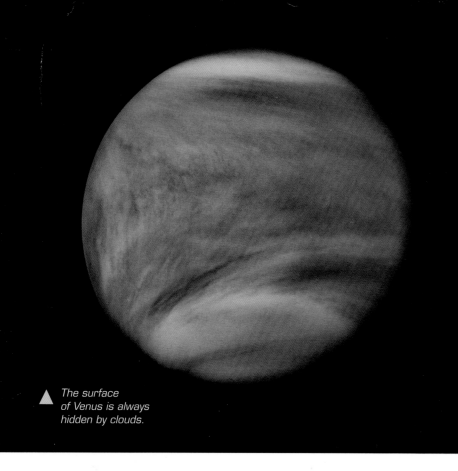

The surface of Venus is always hidden by clouds.

## What's in a Name?

Venus is named after the goddess of love in Roman mythology. Astronomers have named all the different parts of Venus' surface after women in myth and history, including Eve and Aphrodite. Venus is sometimes called "the morning star" or "the evening star" since it **orbits** close to the Sun, it is often seen in the eastern sky at dawn and the western sky at dusk.

## How can we learn about Venus if it's always cloudy?

All the pictures of Venus taken from Earth and in space only show the upper layers of the clouds. To penetrate the thick clouds, we need to use the same instrument that airports do to locate planes on cloudy days: **radar**. The *Magellan* spacecraft orbited Venus between 1990 and 1994 and sent back amazing close-up radar views of Venus.

## Have any spacecraft landed on Venus?

Between 1975 and 1981, four Russian *Venera* robot probes landed on Venus. They managed to survive from 50 minutes to two hours in Venus's deadly environment. Each probe sent back pictures of the surface and lots of information about the planet before being destroyed by the heat and pressure. In 1978, the U.S. *Pioneer* Venus orbiter dropped probes into the atmosphere—one of which survived hitting the surface and sent back signals for over an hour.

GOSH, IT FEELS LIKE WE'RE ON VENUS—I CAN'T BREATHE AND IT FEELS SO HOT IN HERE! HA, HA!

This is a computer-generated image that shows what the surface of Venus might look like if you were looking down upon it from above.

# Earth & Its Moon:
## Our Home Base

Earth is unique among planets we know, thanks to conditions that support life. Its water-covered surface, relatively stable weather, and position close enough to the Sun to provide the right amount of warmth make Earth home to millions of species of animal and plant life. Earth is also the closest planet to the Sun that has a **moon**. Our Moon is the only other world beside Earth on which people have actually walked.

## What does Earth look like from space?

Astronauts report that from space, Earth looks like a beautiful blue marble flecked with white clouds. The daytime side is bright, reflecting the light of the Sun.

## Are there other planets in our solar system that are like Earth?

Several other planets are made of rock and metal like Earth, but no other planet in the solar system is exactly like our own. For example, no other world has liquid water freely flowing on its surface, though Mars might have had some in the past. No other planet has oxygen-rich air as Earth does, nor do other planets enjoy the comfortable temperatures of Earth.

## Why does Earth have a moon?

No one is quite sure. Moons are unusual in the inner solar system, which includes Mercury, Venus, Earth, and Mars. Mercury and Venus have no moons. Mars has two tiny moons that it "stole" from the **asteroid belt**, a zone of rocks between Mars and Jupiter. But it's likely that Earth's Moon had a more violent beginning. Scientists think there was a cosmic collision early in the history of the solar system. They believe that a huge chunk of rock hit Earth and tore a piece out of it. Fragments from both worlds went into orbit and eventually gathered together within the pull of Earth's gravity to form the Moon.

## FAR-OUT FACTS:

**Size:** 7,900 miles (12,800 km) across

**Temperature:** Can range from a low of -92°F (-69°C) near the poles to a high of 136°F (58°C) near the **equator**

**Length of a Year:** 365¼ days. Earth orbits the Sun at 66,000 mph (106,000 km/h).

**Length of a Day:** 24 hours. Earth's equator rotates at a speed of 1,000 mph (1,600 km/h).

**Average Distance from Sun:** 93 million miles (150 million km)

Earth is the only planet with liquid water on its surface.

## Gravity

All matter—from the smallest grains of dust to the largest planets and stars—has **gravity**. Gravity is the force that pulls you to Earth and gives you weight. Without gravity, everything not stuck to the Earth would float off into space. In fact, astronomers think Earth would never have formed without gravity.

## How far away from Earth is the Moon?

On average, the Moon is about 240,000 miles (384,000 km) away from Earth. When the *Apollo* astronauts traveled there in the late 1960s and early 1970s, it took them about 2½ days to travel each way. Billions of years ago, the Moon was closer to Earth, and in the far future, it will be farther away. That's because it's moving about four yards (3.7 meters) away from Earth every century.

In 1984, Astronaut Bruce McCandless became the first spacewalker to use a jet-powered backpack to move around in space.

The Moon is made of rock, so it doesn't shine on its own. The light of the Moon is really sunlight, reflecting back from the Moon's surface.

# Mars:
## The Red Desert Planet

Visible from Earth, the red color of Mars makes it a standout in the sky. Astronomers once thought there might be canals carrying water on Mars, leading some people to conclude that our neighbor planet might be home to intelligent life. No Martian has ever been found, and robot rovers and orbiting telescopes show that Mars is actually a desert planet, with very little or no liquid water. But it does have *frozen* water in its large polar ice caps and may have more underground.

*Phobos, one of the moons of Mars, resembles a potato.*

## Why is Mars red?

The dusty sand of Mars is rich in a chemical called iron oxide. Just as metals such as iron can rust and turn a reddish color on Earth, the iron-rich sands of Mars have turned a rusty red due to exposure to oxygen. As the Martian winds blow fine dust into the sky, the air around Mars can appear to be pink.

## What's it like on Mars?

The Martian landscape includes desert dunes, great fields of craters, giant volcanoes, and deep canyons. Just as on Venus, the air on Mars is made mostly of carbon dioxide, but Martian air is very thin; to find air as thin in Earth's atmosphere, you'd have to go 20 miles (32 km) above the surface. The thin Martian air means that there's very little pressure on Mars. Air pressure is part of what makes water a liquid on Earth because the weight of the air pushes down on the water and keeps it from evaporating. That means it's hard to have liquid water on the surface of the red planet. Also, Mars gets less than half the sunlight of Earth. The thin air is no help in keeping the heat in. So it's much colder on the red planet than on Earth, with average temperatures far below freezing.

## Has Mars always been a cold desert?

No. Scientists think that cold, dusty Mars had thicker air and warmer temperatures billions of years ago. That would have allowed water to flow, creating rivers and lakes. In fact, three robot rovers, *Pathfinder*, *Spirit*, and *Opportunity*, sent by NASA to Mars, have found lots of places where there was once water. But because Mars is small, its gravity is not strong. Without strong gravity, its air escaped into space. Without air pressure, its water evaporated and its temperature fell.

### FAR-OUT FACTS:

**Size:** 4,200 miles (6,800 km) across

**Temperature:** Average temperature is -81°F (-63°C)

**Length of a Year:** 687 Earth days

**Length of a Day:** 24 hours and 40 minutes

**Average Distance from Sun:** 139 million miles (228 million km)

**Fun Fact:** Mount Olympus, the largest volcano on Mars, stands 16 miles (26 km) high—three times the height of Mount Everest.

Mars as seen with the Hubble Space Telescope. Its white polar cap is at the bottom.

## Does Mars have moons?

Mars has two tiny moons, which are probably asteroids that got caught in the planet's gravity. Phobos (Greek for "fear") is only 17 miles (27 km) across, while Deimos (Greek for "panic") is just 10 miles (16 km) across. Up close, they both look like huge potatoes with big pits in them. They are so small that their gravity is very weak. If you threw a ball hard enough from the surface of either of these moons, it would go right into space, escaping the moon's gravity forever.

This painting shows the Mars Exploration Rover on the planet's surface.

The smiley-face crater is in the Argyre region of Mars.

SAY, I LIKE THIS PLANET. I FEEL LESS PRESSURE HERE!

# Jupiter:
## The Great Gas Giant

Jupiter is the largest of all the planets, with more material, or mass, than all the other planets *combined*. It has enough mass that 318 Earths could be made from it! Unlike the rocky inner planets, Jupiter is a gas-and-liquid giant, held together by its gravity, with only a tiny solid core. If you tried to land a spaceship on Jupiter, you'd be pulled down by its gravity and then crushed by its atmosphere—unless you got caught up in the giant winds blowing in its upper atmosphere first.

## FAR-OUT FACTS:

**Size:** 87,000 miles (143,000 km) across. Jupiter is the largest planet.

**Temperature:** Average temperature in the outer atmosphere is -240°F (-150°C).

**Length of a year:** Slightly fewer than 12 Earth years

**Length of a Day:** 10 hours

**Average Distance from Sun:** 480 million miles (778 million km)

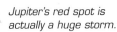

Jupiter's red spot is actually a huge storm.

GAWRSH! IS IT JUST ME OR ARE WE SPINNING FAST?

## What makes Jupiter so windy?

Jupiter's size contributes to its fast speed. This huge ball of gas spins more quickly on its axis than any other planet, giving it a day that's only about ten hours long. This speedy spin causes strong horizontal winds. The rising of heated gases from its core and the sinking of cooling gases from its outer layers also whip up vertical winds. The constant churning causes storms that make the largest hurricanes on Earth look like spring showers!

## What is that huge red spot in the clouds of Jupiter?

The mysterious red spot is a giant storm. This particular storm has been around for centuries. Astronomers have been following it for more than 300 years. The storm has grown bigger and smaller over time, but it hasn't died down yet. At its biggest, it has been as large as *three Earths* placed side by side. The exact reason for the reddish color remains a puzzle. In 2006, astronomers found a "junior red spot" forming right under the giant one.

## What's in a name?

Jupiter is named after the king of the gods in Roman mythology, who was named Zeus in Greek mythology. Jupiter's moons are named after the god's wives and other female friends. (According to various myths, he had a lot of them!)

◄ *Jupiter is by far the largest planet in our solar system. The colors in this photo are exaggerated to make the red spots stand out.*

## Does Jupiter have moons?

Yes, it has at least 63 of them! Jupiter's four giant moons are some of the most interesting worlds we know.

**Io** is a moon with more active volcanoes than any other moon or planet. In fact, so many volcanoes and geysers spew out so much material that astronomers say Io is slowly turning itself inside out. Io's volcanoes can send up plumes of erupted material 180 miles (290 km) high. Some of the material actually escapes Io's gravity and goes into orbit.

**Europa** is the smoothest body in the solar system—a ball of frozen ice with a very complicated system of cracks in it. Scientists think there might be liquid water—and maybe even life—under the ice.

**Ganymede** is the largest known moon in our solar system. At 3,280 miles (5,279 km) across, it is bigger than either Pluto or Mercury. Like Europa, it, too, may have a liquid layer under its icy surface.

**Callisto** is made mainly of ice that's as hard as rock. It has more craters than any of the other big moons, evidence that it has been hit by lots of space debris.

▼ *The four big moons of Jupiter: Io, Europa, Ganymede, and Callisto*

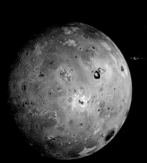
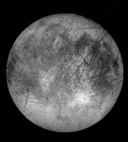

# Saturn:
## King of the Rings

Saturn, like Jupiter, is a giant planet made mostly of gas and liquid, with no solid surface. It contains enough material to make 95 Earths, yet for all its mass, it's not very heavy. If you could find a bathtub big enough to hold it, Saturn would float! What immediately captures our attention most about this planet, however, is its magnificent system of rings. Astronomers have also discovered dozens of moons around Saturn—some of which actually orbit inside the rings!

Mimas with its crater Herschel

### What are Saturn's rings made of?

From far away, the rings of Saturn appear to be solid, but they are actually made of billions and billions of individual icy pieces—some as small as a grain of sand and others as big as a bus. The pieces actually circle Saturn in many thousands of ringlets, which together look like several larger rings from afar. The rings of Saturn are so big, they can reflect quite a bit of sunlight onto the night side of Saturn. The light from the rings is called "ring-shine," just as reflected sunlight from our Moon is called "moonshine."

### How big is the ring system?

Astronomers have discovered seven distinct bands circling Saturn. When scientists identified and named the first three rings, they came up with the names A, B, and C. Not very inspiring! Later astronomers, finding additional rings, were stuck with calling them D, E, F, and G. The rings' names tell the order in which they were found, not the order in which they orbit Saturn.

*HUMMPH! THAT DONALD! HE TOLD ME I HAVE MORE RINGS THAN ANYBODY!*

Together, the three big rings—A, B, and C—are about 40,000 miles (64,000 km) wide but only about 60 feet (20 meters) thick. About 2,000 miles (3,200 km) outside this edge, there is an amazingly narrow ring, called the F ring, which is only about 60 miles (100 km) across and very thin.

This photo shows almost 40,000 miles of Saturn's A, B, and C rings.

### FAR-OUT FACTS:

**Size:** 75,000 miles (120,500 km) across

**Temperature:** Temperatures at the cloudtops of Saturn range from -312°F (-190°C) to -190°F (-125°C).

**Length of a Year:** 29 Earth years

**Length of a Day:** About 10 hours

**Average Distance from Sun:** 885 million miles (1.4 billion km)

**Fun Fact:** If you could float in Saturn's clouds at night, you could read a book by the light of the ringshine.

Saturn has seven rings and 47 moons.

## What's in a Name?

Saturn is named after the Roman god whose special interest was farming. In Greek, this god was called Cronos, and he was the father of Zeus (Jupiter). Cronos led a group of giant older gods called the Titans. The main moons of Saturn are named after various Titans, with the largest one just called Titan.

## What keeps the rings in place?

A **shepherd moon**, called Atlas, keeps the edge of the main ring system sharp as it orbits along the rim and keeps the rings from getting out of line. Atlas is like a shepherd who keeps a flock of sheep from straying beyond a certain point. The F ring stays thin because it has *two* shepherd moons—Prometheus and Pandora— one on each side of it, to keep it in line.

## Are all of Saturn's moons "shepherds"?

No. Among Saturn's 47 moons, there are many that simply orbit the planet outside the realm of the rings. Saturn's largest moon, Titan, is a major world of its own. It has a thicker atmosphere than Earth and is the only moon in our solar system with a thick atmosphere. The outer layer of the atmosphere is very smoggy. A probe called *Huygens* landed on Titan in 2005 and found evidence of rivers and lakes of liquid methane, known on Earth as "swamp gas," that flow among rocks made of frozen water. Another of Saturn's moons, Mimas, is a true celestial survivor: though only about 250 miles (400 km) across, it has an 80-mile-wide (130-km-wide) crater in it, called the Herschel Crater. Astronomers calculate that if the chunk of rock that made it had been just a little bit bigger, it would have cracked the moon apart, breaking it into fragments. Some of Saturn's smaller moons are *inside* its system of rings. A newly discovered moon, only about four miles across, orbits in a thin gap in the A ring. Its gravity creates ripples in the arrangement of the ice chunks that make up the A ring.

The "rocks" of Titan's surface are probably made of frozen water but are as hard as rock.

# Uranus & Neptune:
## The Blue Twins

Uranus and Neptune are cold outer giants, smaller than Jupiter and Saturn, but much bigger than Earth. Since Uranus and Neptune are not visible to the naked eye, they were discovered by astronomers using telescopes. Uranus was discovered in 1781, by William Herschel, a musician and astronomy hobbyist. Neptune was not found until 1846. Only one spacecraft, *Voyager 2*, has ever explored these faraway worlds up close.

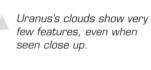

### How are these planets alike?

Both are made of gas and liquid, especially hydrogen and helium, and have methane in their atmospheres. Because they are so far from the Sun, Uranus and Neptune are freezing cold and dark. The length of their days is shorter than Earth's, and their fast spin sets up horizontal weather patterns similar to those on Jupiter and Saturn, although the pattern is much harder to see on Uranus. Both planets have many moons and systems of rings. Their rings are much thinner than Saturn's, and they, too, are guided in their orbits by shepherd moons.

Uranus's clouds show very few features, even when seen close up.

### How are they different?

Uranus stands apart from Neptune and all the planets in the extreme tilt of its axis. Some planets, including Mercury and Jupiter, have an axis that points nearly straight up. Earth's axis is tilted by 23 degrees and Neptune's by 29 degrees. But Uranus has its axis tilted sideways, so that the planet orbits the Sun while lying on its side! For part of the year, Uranus's North Pole faces the Sun, and for part of the year, its South Pole does, making for strange seasons.

The Verona Cliff on Miranda (at right) is 12 miles high.

## FAR-OUT FACTS:

**Size:** Uranus is 32,000 miles (51,200 km) across. Neptune is 31,000 miles (49,500 km) across.

**Temperature:** Temperature at the cloudtops of each planet is -350°F (-212°C).

**Length of a Year:** Uranus's year is 84 Earth years. Neptune's year is 165 Earth years.

**Length of a Day:** A Uranus day lasts 17 hours. A Neptune day is 16 hours.

**Average Distance from Sun:** Uranus orbits 1.8 billion miles (2.9 billion km) from the Sun. Neptune orbits 2.8 billion miles (4.5 billion km) from the Sun.

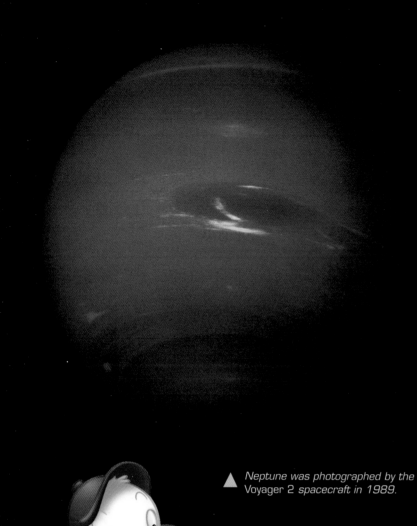

Neptune was photographed by the Voyager 2 *spacecraft* in 1989.

THE ONLY THING BETTER THAN TWINS IS TRIPLETS!

Neptune's moon Triton orbits its planet *backward*.

## Are their moons alike?

No two moons are exactly alike. One of Uranus's moons, Miranda, is often compared to a jigsaw puzzle—with pieces that don't quite fit one another. Miranda's most famous attraction may be the Verona Cliff, which is 12 miles (19 km) high at its highest point— 12 times taller than the sides of Earth's Grand Canyon!

Neptune's biggest and most interesting moon is Triton, which is the only big moon in the solar system that orbits its planet *backward*. Triton is a ball of pink ice. With a temperature of –400°F (–240°C), it's the coldest world our robot probes have ever explored. Triton is slowly approaching Neptune and may break into pieces or fall into Neptune someday. Triton is almost exactly a twin of Pluto in size and in composition.

# Pluto & Beyond:
## Icy Dwarfs

Pluto is the first **dwarf planet** to have been found beyond Neptune. It's different from the outer planets. It's small and solid, more like the inner planets. Plus, it orbits differently than the planets. Pluto has one big moon and at least two tiny ones. But the biggest news is that Pluto seems to have lots of company in its region of space. About a thousand icy objects have recently been found beyond Neptune. At least one of these is bigger than Pluto, and several are almost as big.

## How was this tiny, faraway world discovered?

The astronomer Percival Lowell believed that the orbits of Uranus and Neptune were being affected by an unknown planet. He set out to find this new world, but he died without success. The Lowell Observatory in Arizona, which he started, took up the search, taking many photos of the sky to see if there was anything out there. To scan the photos, they hired a young farm boy named Clyde Tombaugh. He looked at more than 90 *million* points of light on the photos—and, in 1930, he found little Pluto. There is an even stranger twist to this story. It turns out that Pluto has a mass that is so small it could not have affected the orbits of Uranus and Neptune. The discovery of Pluto was a lucky accident, which resulted from people simply looking carefully at many likely places that such a world might be found.

### FAR-OUT FACTS:

**Size:** 1,400 miles (2,260 km) across

**Temperature:** Ranges from –350°F (–213°C) to –370°F (–223° C)

**Length of a Year:** 249 Earth years

**Length of a Day:** More than 6 Earth days

**Average Distance from Sun:** 3.7 billion miles (5.9 billion km)

## What is different about Pluto?

What isn't? At only 1,400 miles across, Pluto is smaller than any of the planets. Even Earth's moon is bigger. Though planets travel in an elliptical, or oval-shaped, orbit, the dwarf planet Pluto's orbit is much more stretched out. Sometimes, Pluto's orbit puts it *inside* the orbit of Neptune, and then it loops out almost two *billion* miles beyond Neptune. And its largest moon, called Charon, is nearly half Pluto's size.

THERE *IS* LIFE ON PLUTO! HE'S GOT FLEAS!

## What's beyond Pluto?

For 65 years, Pluto was the only world we knew beyond Neptune. People wondered if there were more worlds farther out, but we did not have any way to find them. Now, with better instruments, astronomers have found many icy objects out there. It looks like Neptune's strange moon, Triton, as well as Pluto and Charon are all part of a larger family of ice worlds that formed early in the history of the solar system.

This painting shows what Pluto and Charon might look like from one of the tiny moons recently discovered around Pluto.

## What's in a Name?

Pluto was named after the god of the underworld, the world of darkness in Roman mythology, because it is so far from the Sun. The astronomers at the Lowell Observatory also liked the name because the first two letters were the initials of Percival Lowell, the observatory's founder. Charon, Pluto's large moon, is named after the boatman who rowed the dead to Pluto's domain.

## More Worlds

In 2005, astronomers discovered Eris, an icy new world, roughly twice as far from the Sun as Pluto. Although it is very hard to see, it appears to be bigger than Pluto and to have an even stranger orbit. It takes 560 years for this ice world to go around the Sun, and its orbit is tilted even more than Pluto's. Astronomers have also found at least five objects out there that are roughly the size of Charon. Some or all of these will join Pluto as dwarf planets in the outer reaches of the solar system.

# Asteroids & Comets:
## Cosmic Leftovers

In addition to planets and moons, the solar system has smaller chunks of rocky or icy material left over from its early days. These bits of rock and ice orbit the Sun, but are too small to earn the name planet. Astronomers give them the general name Small Solar System Bodies. Within that family are rocky chunks called **asteroids** and icy chunks called **comets**. Both asteroids and comets have crashed into other worlds, sometimes changing them forever.

LEFTOVERS? I'VE HEARD OF THOSE. I'VE JUST NEVER SEEN ANY ON MY PLATE!

Asteroid Gaspra, which is about ten miles long, is shown here in a photo taken with the Galileo space probe's cameras. The colors are slightly enhanced; the asteroid would look a little duller gray to your eyes.

## FAR-OUT FACTS:

**Average Asteroid Belt Distance from Sun:** 250 million miles (400 million km)

**Average Kuiper Belt Distance from Sun:** 3.7 billion miles (6 billion km)

**Average Oort Cloud Distance from Sun:** 5,000 billion miles (8,050 billion km)

## Where do we find asteroids and comets in our solar system?

Most of the asteroids and comets are organized into three special zones. There is an asteroid belt between Mars and Jupiter, which has roughly three quarters of all the asteroids in it. Of the remaining asteroids, some have orbits that bring them near Earth. These are called Earth-crossing asteroids. Beyond Neptune and Pluto, there is a zone of icy comets and ice worlds called the **Kuiper Belt**. And much, farther out there is a huge collection of comets, called the **Oort Cloud**. It is roughly 50,000 times farther from the Sun than Earth is on average—about 5,000 billion miles (8,050 billion km) away.

## How many asteroids and comets are there in our solar system?

No one knows the answer to this question, since we can't see comets or asteroids that are too small or too far away—and that's most of them. Astronomers estimate that there are at least a million asteroids bigger than one-half mile wide. The number of comets is even more impressive. There are probably over *1,000 billion* icy pieces in the Kuiper Belt and Oort Cloud.

## Can spacecraft visit an asteroid?

Yes! Several robot probes have flown by an asteroid, and two have even landed on asteroids. Since asteroids get hit by smaller chunks of rock and ice, they are covered with craters. Some have even been hit so hard that they've broken apart. These pieces might wind up hitting other asteroids or slamming into moons or planets.

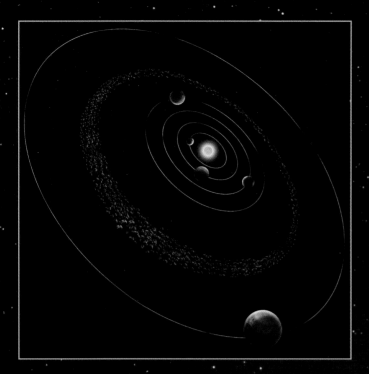

This painting shows the location of the asteroid belt in our solar system.

This is Comet NEAT. The picture shows a patch of sky five times the size of the full Moon.

## What's in a Name?

At first, astronomers named asteroids after women in mythology, but soon the list of asteroids grew too long and they ran out of names. So they began to name asteroids after astronomers and other people who have made life on Earth more interesting. For example, Asteroid 4859 is called Asteroid Fraknoi after the author of this book. And four asteroids are called John, Paul, George, and Ringo, after members of the rock group the Beatles. Comets, on the other hand, are named after the person who first discovers them.

## Asteroids That Hit the Earth

Earth-crossing asteroids sometimes actually hit our planet. If the chunk that hits is really small, it often burns up in Earth's atmosphere. But a bigger chunk can cause a lot of damage. About 50,000 years ago, a 40-yard-wide chunk hit Earth and made a crater about a mile across. It is now a tourist attraction in Arizona, called Meteor Crater. Recently, scientists have found evidence that an asteroid more than 10 miles across hit Earth 65 million years ago. It changed our planet's weather for years, killing about half of the plants and animals that were living then—including the dinosaurs. Astronomers keep track of Earth-crossing asteroids to predict if they're on a collision course with Earth.

# Planets Around Other Stars

### How do astronomers find planets if they can't see them?

The answer is the planet's gravity. As a planet orbits its star, it pulls on the star with its gravity—drawing it first to one side and then to the other. Planets don't have a lot of gravity compared to stars, so their pull is small. Still, as the planet goes around the star, it makes the star wiggle a tiny bit. Imagine a parent whirling a toddler around. The toddler moves in a big circle, but the parent wobbles a bit while turning. Since the early 1990s, astronomers have been building devices to find star wiggles.

### What kind of planets are astronomers finding?

Since the "wiggle method" of locating planets relies on the gravity of the planet, the planets astronomers can find most easily are the ones that pull on their stars with the most gravity. This means that big planets or planets that are close to their stars are the easiest to discover. In fact, the first planets found outside of our solar system were about the size of Jupiter *and* took only a few days to orbit their star. Think about it. Mercury, the planet closest to our Sun, takes 88 days to go around the Sun once. Yet the first planet scientists discovered around another star took only four days! By 2006, astronomers have found about 40 big planets that go around their stars in *ten days or less*. Astronomers call these new kinds of planets "hot Jupiters," because they are so close to their stars, while our Jupiter is much farther out.

The Hubble Space Telescope helps astronomers to see deep into the universe.

### How many planets have been found around other stars?

Astronomers have found more than 200 planets around other stars—and continue to find new ones all the time. None of the new planets have been given names yet because astronomers are still trying to come up with a system for naming these new worlds.

For centuries, sky watchers have wondered if the planets around *our* Sun are the only planets in the universe. Could there be planets around other stars, too? Planets are harder to spot than stars because compared to stars, planets are very dim.

## Don't big planets have to orbit far from their stars?

In our solar system, most of the smaller planets are near the Sun, and the big ones are farther away. But it seems that's not the only way planets can be arranged around a star. Astronomers think that the hot Jupiters may have formed farther out (like our Jupiter), but they may have slid inward during the early days of their star systems' creation.

## Are astronomers finding planets farther out from their stars, too?

Yes, indeed, scientists now know of more than 50 planets that take longer than two Earth years to orbit their stars. (In our solar system, these planets would be farther than Mars is from the Sun.) Astronomers have to watch a star wiggle until the planet has gone completely around to be sure of what they are seeing. So if a planet takes five days to complete its orbit, the scientists will find it by watching the star wiggle for five days. But if a planet takes 30 years to go around, it will take 30 years before they are sure of their results. So it should not be a surprise that scientists are finding the close, quick-orbiting planets first. But astronomers think the slow ones are there, too. Stay tuned!

## Do all stars have planets?

This is the big question. Astronomers now know some stars have planets. They have checked other nearby stars carefully, and found that the stars don't have any big planets. These stars could have small planets, but astronomers can't yet find the smaller wiggles they cause. Many astronomers think that a majority of stars have planets. Like so much else in science, the only way to find out the answer to this question is to do more observing.

# Stars

▲ Star birth

▲ The Sun      ▲ Constellation Orion      ▲ Crab Nebula      ▲ Star cluster

If you stood outdoors on a perfectly clear night, with no clouds to block your view and no city lights to compete with the brightness of the sky, you would see about 3,000 stars in the sky. That sounds like a lot, but it's a small number compared to the 200 *billion* or so stars in our galaxy.

As you watch the twinkling lights, you're seeing the same amazing star show that ancient people saw. And you probably have some of the same questions that they did. *What are stars? What makes them shine? How far away are they? Are they all the same?*

Thanks to modern instruments, we know so much more about stars than the ancients could even imagine. We've learned that our own Sun is a star. It just looks brighter and larger because we are so much closer to it. We've watched stars being born, living, and dying. We've been able to find the remnants of some stars that have died—white dwarfs and black holes. We've even found planets orbiting around 200 or so stars in our galaxy.

What exactly *is* a star? A star is a huge ball of gas hundreds of thousands of miles across that shines under its own power. Stars are the *only* celestial objects that make their own light. Planets shine by reflecting the light of their stars.

A star can live for millions or billions of years. By observing many thousands of different stars at different stages of growth and decline, we can piece together their life stories: their dramatic births; their long periods of stability; and their midlife crises, when they grow bigger around the middle and brighter, too— just like some people! Finally, we can see stars dying—sometimes peacefully, sometimes "kicking and screaming" in great explosions.

Unlike the ancients, we even know that without the light and heat of stars, life in the universe would not be possible.

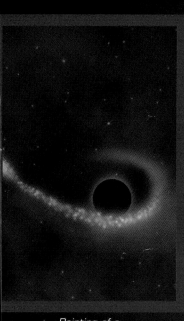

Painting of a black hole

# Constellations: Maps to the Stars

Try to visualize the world without the help of a map. Could you figure out how far Moscow is from London or which way to travel to get from San Francisco to New York? It wouldn't be easy! For centuries, mapmakers have charted areas of Earth to help us navigate from place to place. Like mapmakers, ancient astronomers made maps of the sky to mark the position of certain **stars**. Modern astronomers, too, have mapped the patterns of stars, called **constellations**.

## What is a constellation?

A constellation is a group of stars that form a pattern in a certain part of the sky. Ancient astronomers identified constellations by connecting bright stars to imagine dot-to-dot pictures. When looking at the group of stars shown in the photo to the right, for example, the ancient Greeks saw a hunter, whom they named Orion, after a character in their mythology. Modern astronomers needed a map that included *all* the stars, not just the bright ones that made interesting patterns. So, they divided the sky into boxes to help sky watchers identify different sections of the heavens. They named each box after a famous ancient star pattern found within it.

## Are all the constellations the same size and shape?

No. Just as countries are not the same size or shape, the 88 constellation boxes are different shapes and sizes. When you see the constellations on a globe, picture the Earth inside and the globe as the sky all around it.

▲ Ancient astronomers imagined that this star pattern formed the outline of a hunter, which they named Orion. The three stars across the middle form Orion's belt, from which hangs his sword. The top left star is his shoulder.

## FAMOUS STARS:

### Polaris

Polaris is the name given to the North Star. Polaris is almost exactly above Earth's North Pole. It's part of an asterism called the Little Dipper and of a constellation called Ursa Minor, or the Little Bear. Polaris shines 2,200 times more brightly than our Sun. It's so far away, however, that it takes light from the star 450 years to reach Earth!

## How many constellations are there?

Modern astronomers have mapped 88 boxes, or constellations. This is similar to the way mapmakers and political leaders divided the continental United States into 48 boxes, called states.

ACCORDING TO MY CAREFUL CALCULATIONS, THE NORTH STAR IS TO THE NORTH!

The Big Dipper

## The Big Dipper

The Big Dipper, perhaps the most famous star pattern, is part of the constellation Ursa Major, the big bear. Such smaller groups of stars within constellations are called **asterisms**. To many observers, this asterism looks like a large spoon for serving soup, which is why we call it a big dipper. In some parts of the United States, the Big Dipper used to have the nickname "the drinking gourd." Before and during the U.S. Civil War, escaping slaves followed "the drinking gourd" northward to freedom.

## Are the stars in a constellation together in space?

No. Most of the time they are not. Constellations are just patterns that the stars happen to form in the sky. The stars in a typical star pattern are at very different distances from us and are not connected in any way.

## Why don't we see the same constellations in the same place in the sky all the time?

Earth spins around once every 24 hours. It seems to us that the sky turns and the constellations move around, but it's really our planet that is moving. (You get the same effect when you sit on a bus. It looks like the buildings that line the street are moving backward, but you know it's really the bus that's moving). Also, Earth goes around the Sun once a year. As we move around the Sun, we see different stars in the night sky. Many constellations visible in the summer are not visible during the winter.

I CAN'T FIND THE BIG DIPPER.

WELL, WHERE DID YOU SEE IT LAST?

As the Earth turns, the stars appear to turn. This photograph was taken over a period of 150 minutes. In that time, Earth was turning, causing each star to appear in the photograph as a line instead of a point.

# The Sun: Our Nearest Star

The Sun is 93 million miles from Earth, but that's pretty close for a star. Having a star close by is very handy. Astronomers can monitor it with instruments on Earth and in space to get to know its behavior much better than they can any other, more distant, star. And, of course, without this particular star, there would be no solar system, no planet Earth, no astronomers, no you. It's easy to understand why many ancient cultures worshipped this star.

*I STAYED UP ALL NIGHT LOOKING FOR THE SUN. THEN, FINALLY, IT DAWNED ON ME... .*

## FAMOUS STARS:

### The Sun

- Light takes about eight minutes to travel from the Sun to Earth. So the sunlight you see is eight minutes old.

- Our Sun has enough material to make 333,000 Earths.

- If you weigh a hundred pounds on Earth, you'd weigh 2,800 pounds on the surface of the Sun.

- The temperature in the center of the Sun is estimated to be 28 million degrees Fahrenheit (Ouch!).

- The Sun boils off 10 million tons of material each year, releasing it in a kind of wind that blows through the solar system.

## What makes the Sun different from other stars?

Not much, really. It's medium-sized for a star—864,000 miles in diameter. It has a medium temperature for a star—about 10,000°F (6,000°C) on its surface. And it's middle-aged for a star of its type—about 5 billion years old. What makes it special to us is that it's close enough to provide the warmth and light needed to make life on Earth possible.

## What's the Sun made of?

Like all stars, our Sun is mostly made of two gases—hydrogen and helium—the simplest types of gases in nature. Most of the universe is, in fact, made of these two elements. The Sun has many other kinds of **atoms**, too, but only in tiny amounts compared to the atoms of hydrogen and helium.

## Does the Sun ever change?

The Sun, like other stars, has a life span and "seasons." Astronomers have found, for example, that the Sun goes through an 11-year cycle during which its surface gets more and less active. During the active part of this cycle, the sun has more **sunspots**—or cooler, dark areas—than it does during less active phases.

The Sun's surface often bubbles and erupts.

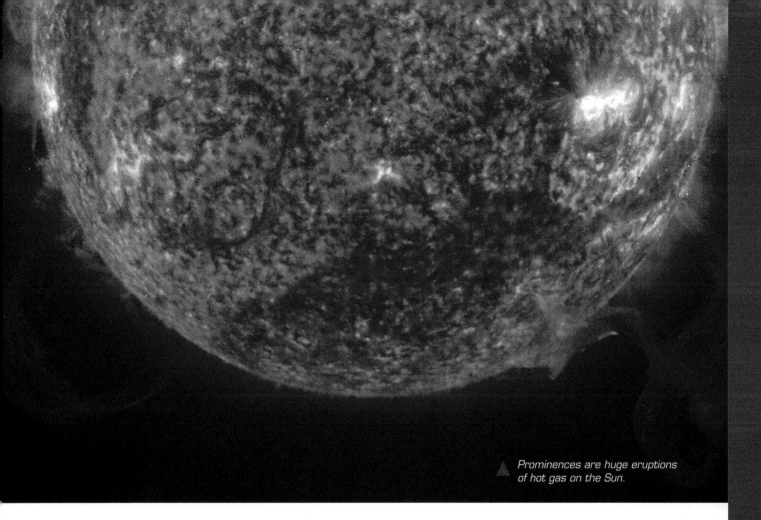

Prominences are huge eruptions of hot gas on the Sun.

## What happens during the active phase of the Sun's cycle?

The bubbling surface of the Sun gets more active. Great plumes of hot gas arch upward and sometimes even erupt into space. These great arches are called **prominences**. You can see how dramatic they are in the pictures on these pages. Scientists have tracked the sunspot cycle for hundreds of years. The last peak in Sun activity was between the years 2000 and 2002, so the next peak should come in 2011 and last until about 2013.

## How big are sunspots?

Some sunspots are actually bigger than Earth, but they look small in comparison to the Sun.

WE WORK THE NIGHT SHIFT, SO WE'RE USUALLY TOO TIRED TO SPOT THE SUN

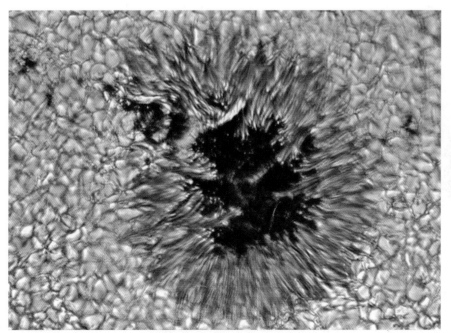

Close-up of a sunspot

# A Star Is Born

It's not easy to become a star. To begin with, there needs to be raw material—gas and dust. There also needs to be a place to grow. For stars, those places are inside giant clouds of raw material in space. Finally, there needs to be a set of conditions to get the process going—gravity and heat—to transform the raw materials into a shining star. Gravity pulls the cloud materials together. As the materials fall toward the middle of the cloud, they get hotter and hotter.

## What do stars need to be born?

Just as babies need the nourishment provided by their mothers before they're born, stars need a nourishing environment to help them get started. Astronomers now know that stars begin in huge, dark clouds of gas and dust. These are the great nurseries of space. The dust and gas are drawn together by gravity, forming the first stage of a star.

## How can we see inside a dark cloud?

Because they're dark, clouds of gas and dust are generally hard to see. Most of the time they are invisible. But once stars have been born in a cloud, the young stars shine brightly. They light up the parts of the cloud near them and make the cloud easier to see. Such a shining cloud of gas and dust is called a **nebula**. A nebula that is making new stars can be very beautiful, as you can see in the pictures on these pages.

▲ This star-forming region shows a group of young, hot blue stars in the middle.

▼ The Horsehead Nebula is in the constellation of Orion.

## FAMOUS STARS:

### The Horsehead Nebula

The Horsehead Nebula is one of the most famous regions where dust and gas are gathering together to make stars. It's a huge pillar of dusty raw material, in front of a reddish cloud of glowing gas. The distance from the "horse's nose" to the "mane" on its back is about two light-years.

The Orion Nebula is the best known starbirth nebula.

## Star Birth in Orion

The Orion Nebula is about 1,500 **light-years** away from Earth in the constellation of Orion. Ancient astronomers imagined that the nebula looked like a spot of blood on the sword of Orion the hunter. The nebula is a glowing patch on a much larger cloud of dark dust and gas. Inside the glowing region, we see hundreds and hundreds of newborn stars. The energy of these baby stars makes the cloud glow and also pushes it apart. With the Hubble Space Telescope, astronomers have found some small, dusty disks inside this nebula. These look just like what our Sun and planets must have looked like five billion years ago when *our* solar system was first forming.

## What happens inside a nebula?

Closer to the center of the cloud, where the gas and dust in the nebula are a little thicker, gravity pulls the materials together. Soon you have a blob of collapsing stuff. (*Blob* and *stuff* are some of the fun words astronomers like to use!) The blob gets hotter as gravity pulls it together. As more material falls on it from the outer cloud, it gets bigger and hotter in the middle. Astronomers call this the **protostar** stage in the life of a star, just as inventors call a new design a *prototype*. Because protostars form within dark clouds, they are usually hidden from our view.

WE'RE THE LATEST PROTOTYPES OF THE CHILD DETECTION AGENCY.

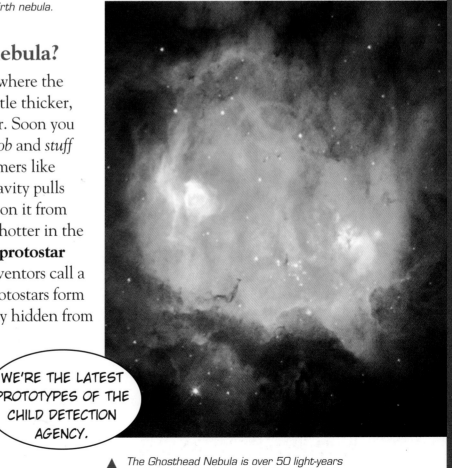

The Ghosthead Nebula is over 50 light-years across. The two glowing "eyes" are places in which hot young stars have already been born.

# Star Light, Star Bright

It's clear to see that the Sun glows bright yellow. Most of the other stars we see are too dim to show their colors. But through telescopes scientists have found some interesting differences among them when it comes to color. Some stars, astronomers now know, are red or orange. Others are blue or a shade of purple. No matter what their color, stars create their own light, a light that can glow for billions of years. The color of a star can tell you its age and health.

## What gives a star its color?

A star's color comes from its temperature. Red stars are relatively cool, with surface temperatures of "only" about 3,100°F (1,700°C). Our yellow Sun's surface is at about 10,000°F (6,000°C). Blue or violet stars are very hot—their surface temperatures can reach about 90,000°F (50,000°C). A helpful way of remembering the color spectrum is the "name" ROY G. BIV. Each letter of this make-believe character's name stands for a color: *red, orange, yellow, green, blue, indigo,* or *violet.* Stars with colors at the beginning of the name are cooler than stars whose colors are at the end.

> PERSONALLY, I PREFER SHADES OF BLUE AND VIOLET.

### FAMOUS STARS:

**The Sun:**

- If we could capture just one second of all the Sun's light and use it on Earth, we would have enough power to satisfy all the energy needs of human civilization for the next 120,000 years!

- The average household bulb uses 40 to 100 watts of energy. The Sun has a wattage of 400,000,000,000,000,000, 000,000,000.

## Are stars on fire?

No. Fire is what happens when fuels like wood or coal get hot and burn. But fire needs oxygen to burn, and there is little oxygen in stars. Remember: stars are made mainly of the gases hydrogen and helium. Also, there is no solid fuel in a star—it's all gas. If a star such as our Sun *did* burn solid fuel, it would have consumed all of its fuel in a short time, in about 10,000 years or so.

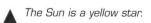

▲ *The Sun is a yellow star.*

The energy from hot newborn stars has made a hole in the center of the Rosette Nebula.

## If stars aren't on fire, what makes them shine?

Stars are huge. Remember the Sun has enough material to make 333,000 Earths! And many other stars are even larger than the Sun. The gravity of all the material in a star squeezes inward very tightly. This means that the middle of a star—the part astronomers call its core—is very hot and under great pressure. The core of a star can reach temperatures of millions of degrees. Once the temperature reaches 18 million degrees Fahrenheit (10 million degrees Celsius), something far more amazing than burning can happen. It's called **fusion**.

*Compared to the Earth, the Sun is very large.* ▶

## Fusion

Are you ready for a minilesson in atomic energy? Good! This one's about a nuclear process called fusion. Here's how fusion works: when under pressure, atoms, which are the main building blocks of all elements, can bang together with so much force that their insides get rearranged. The main part of every atom is called its **nucleus**. When the nuclei of two atoms collide, they combine to form a new element. For example, inside the Sun, superhot hydrogen atoms bang into one another so hard that they create an element called helium. (Yes, that's the gas that keeps balloons flying.) This fusion process releases energy each time it happens. The energy from the fusion of countless atoms causes stars to shine brightly and keeps them glowing for billions of years. Humans have learned how to fuse hydrogen atoms together, creating bombs whose explosions are miniversions of those that take place inside a star. Like all knowledge, the secrets of fusion need to be used wisely.

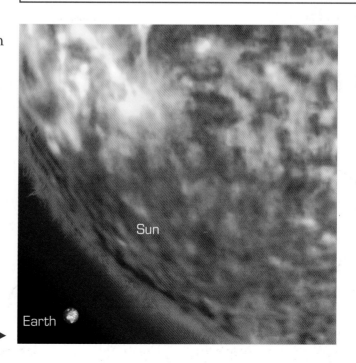

Sun

Earth

# Red Giants

Astronomers say that a star is "born" when it starts shining with its own fusion energy. And as long as it has hydrogen and enough heat in its core for fusion, the star will have a stable life. But as a star gets old, the process of fusion slows because the star's hot hydrogen begins to run out. The star gets weaker without the fuel it needs to perform fusion and goes into a state of crisis. During that crisis, the star swells up and becomes huge.

## How long do most stars live?

The life span of a star depends on how much material it has. Surprisingly, stars that have a lot of material have a shorter life span. And stars with less material live much longer. Stars that have enough gas to make dozens of our Suns will live only a few million years because they consume their fuel very quickly. Stars that have half as much material as our Sun can live over a hundred billion years because they consume their hydrogen more slowly.

## What happens to a star when its hydrogen fuel runs out?

When all the fuel hot enough for fusion runs out, the star enters its crisis period. It briefly swells up and gets much bigger in size than it was during most of its life. As it grows larger, the star's outside cools down, and it turns red. Astronomers call such stars **red giants**. Red giants never return to full health. They continue to leak some of their material into space and eventually die.

*A cluster of stars at the bottom right of this picture includes several bright red giants.* ▶

## FAMOUS STARS:

### Betelgeuse

This is probably the best known red giant in the sky. It looks bright and red to the naked eye, which is pretty amazing given that it is 430 light-years away. Betelgeuse (pronounced "beetle-juice") is 650 times larger than the Sun. If our Sun were the size of Betelgeuse, its outer edge would stretch beyond the orbit of Mars! Betelgeuse has a huge atmosphere around it, making it look fuzzy. The Hubble Space Telescope took a great photo of it a few years ago.

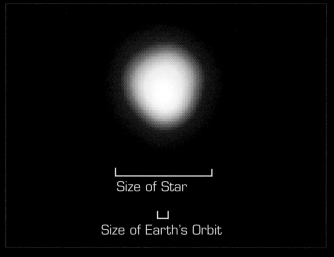

Size of Star

Size of Earth's Orbit

## Star Names

The brightest stars got the attention of early astronomers, who gave them special names based on what they looked like. Sirius, the brightest star in our sky, has a name that means "the scorched one" in Greek. The name of the star Betelgeuse comes from the Arabic "bet al jauza," which means "the right hand of the central one."

In 1725, a British astronomer started giving the brightest stars in each constellation a number. So Betelgeuse is also called 58 Orionis, which means it's the 58th star in the constellation of Orion. Later, astronomers using telescopes started making catalogs of less prominent stars, and these are known by their catalog numbers. An example is HD149026. This long number shows that modern astronomers have far surpassed the ancients in the number of stars that they know of and have long since run out of poetic names to apply to them.

▲ *On the top, we see a Hubble Space Telescope photo of the red giant Betelgeuse. Below this is the constellation figure of Orion. Betelgeuse is the bright star at top left.*

▼ *Comparing a red giant to our Sun*

Our Sun

I'M A BLUE GIANT!

Red Giant

## Will the Sun ever become a red giant?

All stars become red giants eventually, and our Sun is no exception. Astronomers have been measuring the Sun's fuel and the way it has been used up so far. They think that the Sun still has about 5 to 7 billion years to go before it weakens and dies. So you have plenty of time to finish your homework. When our Sun becomes a red giant, its outer edge will pass the orbit of Mars.

# White Dwarfs & Supernovae

Once a star becomes a red giant, it's heading for the end of its life, which could take millions or even billions of years. Not all red giants die in the same way. Some will shrink and shed their outer layers, glowing brightly before fading away. Other dying stars will explode with a ferocious force, and their light will linger for centuries after they're gone. The way a star dies depends on how much material it contains.

## What happens to red giants?

The red-giant crisis in a star's life ends when the star runs out of hydrogen and finds new fuel to use for fusion. The star begins to fuse helium atoms into another kind of atom called **carbon**. This process produces a lot of energy and makes the star stable—but only for a while.

▼ *A dying star loses its outer layers.*

GOOD THING WE HAVE NIGHT JOBS. WE'LL NEVER MISS THE SUN.

## How will our Sun die?

The temperature that a star's core must reach to fuse helium into carbon is a mind-boggling 180 *million* degrees Fahrenheit (100 million degrees Celsius). Only the very center of the Sun will get this hot. This stage will last about a hundred million years, which, considering the 10-billion-year life span of the Sun, is not a very long time. After all the helium atoms that are hot enough have fused into carbon atoms, no further fusion will be possible. The Sun will then have a "last gasp" and shed its outer layer. The rest of the Sun will collapse, until the once-huge star is only a little bigger than Earth.

▼ *This cloud of gas is all that remains of a star that exploded in the year 1054. It is called the Crab Nebula.*

## FAMOUS STARS:

### The Crab Nebula

One day, in the summer of 1054, people around the world woke up to an amazing sight: a bright new star was visible in the constellation of Taurus the bull. The star could even be seen faintly during the daytime! It was a supernova—a huge star exploding at the end of its life. Today, nearly a thousand years later, we can still see the gas from the explosion moving outward. Through small telescopes, the exploded cloud reminds some people of the shape of a crab.

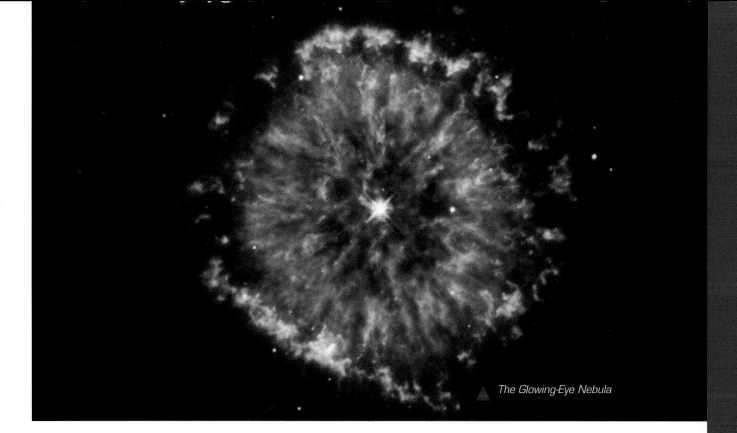

The Glowing-Eye Nebula

## What happens to a star after it dies?

At the end, stars like the Sun collapse until their insides begin to act more like solids than gases. They are tiny, compressed objects by then, more like a planet in size. Because being squeezed makes them white hot, astronomers call such dead stars **white dwarfs**. A million-mile-wide star can shrink to a 20,000 mile–wide white dwarf, which means that the gravity on the surface of the star is extremely strong. A person who weighs 100 pounds on Earth would weigh 100 million pounds on a white dwarf! White dwarfs have temperatures of tens of thousands of degrees, but they have no new source of energy inside them. So, as millions of years pass, a white dwarf cools down, like an ember after a fire. Finally, it becomes a **black dwarf**—invisible against the blackness of space but still packed with most of the material it had before it became a red giant.

## Do all stars die as white dwarfs?

Most do, but a few stars that contain a lot of material have a more dramatic end. After the red-giant crisis, these stars find other kinds of fusion to keep them going for a while. For example, they fuse carbon and helium into an atom called oxygen—the gas we breathe. But eventually, the huge star becomes unstable, and it explodes. Such a star explosion is called a **supernova**. Supernovae are rare, but when one happens, it can be so bright that the star briefly outshines the billions of other stars in its home galaxy.

## What does a dying star look like?

When a star like the Sun sheds its outer layer, it spreads out and can be quite beautiful. The pictures on this page show you some intriguing "last gasp" shells around dying stars. Such a glowing shell is called a nebula, which is the same name given to all glowing clouds of dust and gas in space, including the clouds of dust in which stars are born.

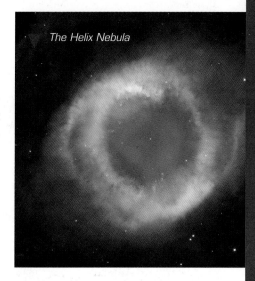

The Helix Nebula

# Black Holes

When it comes to the death of stars, nature has one more surprise up its sleeve. Every once in a while, a "superstar" forms—a star that, at the end of its life, might have 15, 50, or even 100 times as much material as our Sun. When these stars die, something amazing happens. Nothing in the universe can stop the gravity of this huge star from collapsing it. Our theories of gravity tell us the star will fall in forever! Such a collapsed star is called a **black hole**.

## What happens when a star collapses?

When a star collapses under its own weight, all of its material gets squeezed into a smaller and smaller ball. As it shrinks, the surface of the star is now much, much closer to its center. As a result, the force of its gravity at the surface is far stronger than it was when the star was larger.

## How do we measure gravity in a collapsing star?

We can measure the gravity by figuring out how much speed we would need to get away from the star. The greater the gravity,

the greater the **escape speed**. The escape speed from our Sun is over a million miles per hour. But as a dying star collapses, the increasing gravity makes it harder and harder to escape. So the escape speed goes up and up. At some point, the speed needed to get away from a collapsing star becomes faster than 670 million miles per hour (1,080 million kilometers per hour)—that's the speed of light. When the escape speed is greater than the speed of light, nothing, *not even light*, can get away. So the collapsed star is called a black hole.

### FAMOUS STARS:

#### Cygnus X-1

The best known black hole is found in the constellation of Cygnus the Swan. It consists of a bright living star that looks like it's orbiting nothing. From the middle of that "nothing," telescopes pick up X-rays coming from a swirling disk of material that is falling into a black hole. The way the living star moves around tells us that the black hole has roughly 16 times as much material in it as our Sun has. This is just the sort of big star that would make a black hole.

## What would happen if you fell into a black hole?

Falling into a black hole would be a once-in-a-lifetime experience! You could never get out to tell anyone what you found inside. And, as you fell in, the great gravity near the black hole would stretch you until you looked like a thin noodle. Ouch!

## Can one black hole eat another black hole?

Yes! When two black holes meet, they can join together to form a bigger black hole. In fact, anything that comes too close to a black hole can get gobbled up.

MIKE, WE PICKED THE WRONG DOOR THIS TIME!

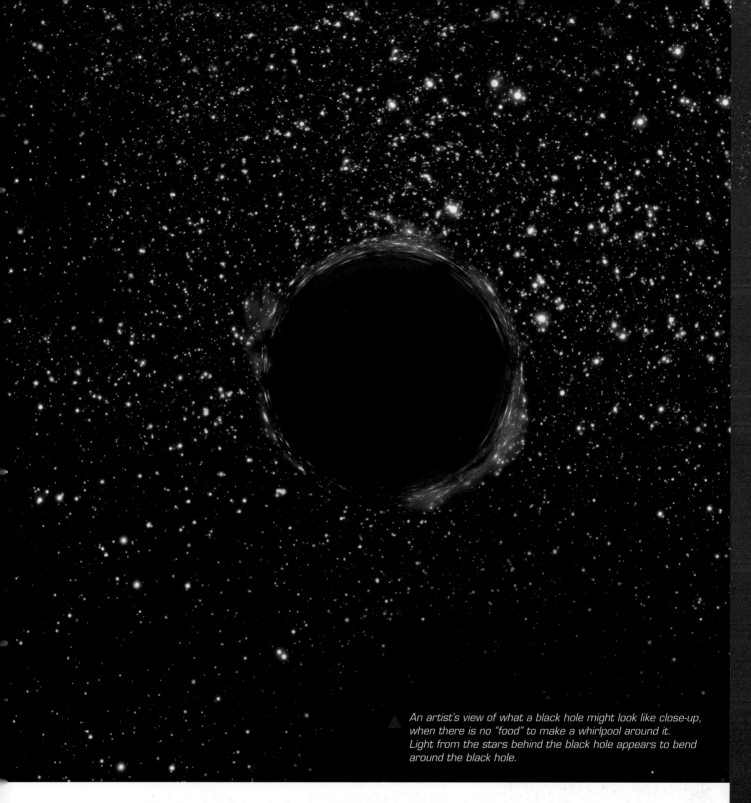

*An artist's view of what a black hole might look like close-up, when there is no "food" to make a whirlpool around it. Light from the stars behind the black hole appears to bend around the black hole.*

## How can we find a black hole if it is black and space is black, too?

If a black hole exists by itself, it is just about impossible to find it from far away. But many stars come in pairs that orbit each other. Imagine that one star in a close pair becomes a black hole and the other becomes a red giant. As the red giant's outer edge expands, it moves closer to the black hole. Then the black hole's gravity can begin to eat away at the living star, pulling its material in. A kind of whirlpool forms around the black hole. Inside it, the atoms of gas from the red giant that are being pulled into the black hole rub together. The friction makes them extremely hot. This causes the whirlpool of gas to glow—not with light, but with waves called X-rays. These X-rays show that the black hole is slowly eating away at its neighboring star.

# Star Pairs & Clusters

Our Sun is a single star, living out its life surrounded by just its family of planets. But this may not have been true when the Sun was born. It's possible that our Sun, like most stars, was born as part of a group of stars. In some cases, just a few stars form together. Sometimes, over a 100,000 stars can be born at the same time. Astronomers have found such groups of stars, called **star clusters**, all around the sky.

▲ A picture of the Alpha Centauri star system taken not with visible light but with heat rays. The light of the stars blends together.

## What happens if two stars form together?

Stars form from spinning clouds of gas and dust. When a pair of stars form near each other, they will pull on each other with gravity. They can settle down into an orbit in which they go around each other. Such two-star systems are called binary stars. Some binary stars have wide orbits, circling each other at a great distance. But others orbit so close to each other that the two stars actually exchange material. When binary stars die, their remnants will often continue to orbit each other forever.

## FAMOUS STARS:

### Alpha Centauri

The nearest star to us outside of our solar system is Alpha Centauri. It is a double star, with two stars orbiting around each other. There is a third star, called Proxima Centauri, lurking some distance away from the two main stars, and astronomers are not sure if Proxima Centauri is just passing by or part of the family. The entire triple system is 4.3 light-years away. So light from Alpha Centauri takes only 4 ⅓ years to reach us. At the speed our rockets currently are able to travel, however, it would take about 100,000 years to cover this distance.

## Can binary stars have planets around them?

Astronomers think it is harder to fit planets into systems with more than one star. But it's not impossible. Scientists have already discovered planets in both a double- and triple-star system. If a planet sticks close to its star, it can survive even when other nearby stars are pulling on it.

▼ The Hubble Space Telescope peers into the center of a very crowded globular cluster called Omega Centauri and sees an amazing number of stars.

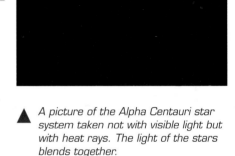

Globular cluster M92

CLUSTERS ALWAYS TRAVEL TOGETHER—JUST LIKE WE DO!

## How are stars arranged into groups?

There are two different kinds of star groups. Open clusters are loose groups of stars, with dozens to thousands of stars in them. Globular clusters, on the other hand, are much more crowded groups. They can have as many as a million stars. Such packed groups of stars usually form round or globe shapes, which is how they get their name.

## What would it be like to live in a globular cluster?

In the middle of a globular cluster, stars are much closer together than stars in our area. If you lived on a planet near the middle of a crowded globular cluster, your night sky would be very different from Earth's. Even when your sun went down, there would be so many nearby bright stars that the night would never get dark!

# The Faraway Stars

Distances to close objects in space can be measured directly. By bouncing a laser beam off a big piece of metal that astronauts left behind on the Moon's surface, scientists measured the distance to the Moon *within inches*! But the stars are really far away, and they don't reflect! And no one would ever be able to leave a reflective tool on any of them. So scientists had to devise other ways to measure the vast distances in space.

## How can we measure distances to the stars?

For stars that are not too far away, astronomers use something they call the **parallax shift** (see box on next page). They look at the same star from two different places to calculate its distance. For example, they might look at a star in the springtime when Earth is at a certain point in its orbit around the Sun. Then they will look at the same star in the autumn, when Earth is at the opposite point in its orbit. Stars that have a small parallax shift are farther away than the stars that have a large parallax shift. To get accurate measurements of parallax, astronomers have sent spacecraft into orbit above Earth's atmosphere. From up there they can measure the parallax shift more accurately than from Earth's surface. Using this method, astronomers can measure distances up to about 600 light-years. For stars much farther away than that, scientists use a different method to measure distances.

## DISTANCES TO FAMOUS STARS FROM EARTH:

These are distances to some famous stars. Remember: one light-year is about 6 *thousand billion* miles.

| Proxima Centauri | Nearest star | 4.3 light-years |
|---|---|---|
| Sirius | Brightest star in sky | 8.6 light-years |
| Epsilon Eridani | Nearest star with known planet | 10.5 light-years |
| Vega | Bright summer star | 25 light-years |
| Arcturus | Nearby red giant | 37 light-years |

## How do we measure the distance to stars that are farther away?

There is a special kind of star called a **Cepheid** that gets a little brighter and a little dimmer on a regular schedule. Almost a century ago, astronomers figured out how to measure the distance of such stars from the way they change their brightness. Cepheids can be found all over the universe, and astronomers have used them to measure distances out to 60 *million* light-years.

## Do closer stars look brighter than faraway stars?

Sometimes, but not always. Ancient astronomers thought that all the stars were the same. They believed that if a star looked brighter then it must be closer to Earth. But today's astronomers know stars are *not* all the same. Some are much bigger and shine more brightly than the Sun. Others seem brighter because they *are* closer. So when scientists see a bright star, they don't know if it looks bright because it shines more or because it's closer—or maybe a bit of both—until they can actually measure its distance.

Andromeda

Perseus

Auriga

Triangulum

Aries

▲ *The star in the very middle is Proxima Centauri, part of the nearby Alpha Centauri system of stars.*

## The Parallax Shift: How Astronomers Measure Distances in the Galaxy

You can tell how far away something is by looking at it from two different angles. Try this experiment to see for yourself.

- Stand 10 feet away from a wall.
- Hold a pencil in front of your nose. Close your right eye. Make a mental note of where on the wall the pencil appears to be.
- Now, open your right eye and close the left one. What seems to happen to the position of the pencil? Did you find that it seemed to have shifted when seen from one eye and then the other?

- Next, hold the pencil at arm's length. Close one eye and then the other. When you held the pencil at arm's length, did it seem to shift less?

This shift you saw is called parallax. You could estimate the distance of the pencil from your nose from the amount of parallax shift. Astronomers use the same idea to measure how far away stars are by looking at a star from two different positions of the Earth.

MY STAR IS BOUND TO GET BRIGHTER ANY DAY NOW!

# Stars and Life on Earth

## What are the ingredients for life on Earth?

All matter is made up of microscopic pieces called atoms. There are many different kinds of atoms, from very simple ones like hydrogen and helium, to complex ones like lead and uranium. Life as we know it needs some special kinds of atoms, including carbon, oxygen, and nitrogen. And these atoms need to combine to form **molecules**, which are made up of more than one atom. For example, an important molecule for life is methane, which is made up of a carbon atom joined to four hydrogen atoms.

## Where did the ingredients for life on Earth come from?

When the universe began, it was made up of only hydrogen and helium, the two simplest atoms in nature. There was no carbon, no oxygen, no gold—none of the atoms we humans especially know and love on Earth. Where did these more complex atoms from? They were made by stars!

## How do stars make atoms?

The process of nuclear fusion batters atoms together with such immense force that they form new elements. So it is the stars that build up new atoms, such as carbon, oxygen, and nitrogen. Later in their lives, stars release some of the newly made atoms into space. Sometimes, they do it peacefully, as when red giants shed their outer layers. Sometimes they do it violently, as when supernovae explode. But either way, the stars recycle their atoms. New stars and planets form from the materials released by old stars. These new stars and planets will then include the atoms the older stars made. Our Sun and its planets have carbon, oxygen, gold, and many other atoms from earlier generations of stars.

Life needs the right ingredients and the right conditions to form and survive. Earth is not too hot and not too cold, and has a thick atmosphere, which gives it the right air pressure to allow water to exist as a liquid. Earth's solid surface lets water collect in lakes, rivers, and oceans, and this available water helped to get life started and allows it to survive.

## Do all the atoms in my body come from stars?

All the atoms besides hydrogen and helium that are in you and everyone else are the result of the fusion that took place in stars that lived and died before the Sun was ever born. You might say that life on Earth literally comes from stardust. We are all amazing products of the workings of the universe.

## The Murchison Meteorite

In September 1969, a rock from space fell to Earth near the town of Murchison, Australia, breaking into many pieces. When scientists looked inside the rocks, they found **amino acids**—complicated molecules that are the building blocks of proteins. Not only did the rock from space have this key building block of life, but the structure of some of those amino acids was different from the ones we find in you, your dog, a cactus, or any other living thing on Earth. So scientists believe that at least some of those amino acids were made in space. This suggests that the steps leading to life may already be happening around other stars.

▼ *A scientist holds a small piece of the Murchison meteorite.*

## Could atoms combine to make life on planets around other stars?

That's one of the biggest questions in all of astronomy. Astronomers have found the atoms needed for life in many star systems. And they now know that many other stars have planets. So astronomers do think that life could start in other places if the conditions are right.

# The Universe & Its Galaxies

▲ Colliding galaxies

▲ Sombrero Galaxy
▲ Painting of the Milky Way
▲ Egg Yolk Galaxy
▲ Painting of a black hole

Imagine this scene: the school bell rings, and everyone leaves the building at the same time. Some kids start to walk home. Others hop onto their bicycles and pedal away, moving more quickly than the walkers. Still others get into school buses and drive away, zipping past the walkers and the bikers. Now imagine that five minutes after everyone has left—but before anyone has reached home yet—a photographer riding in a helicopter takes a photo of the area around the school.

The photo would show that the kids who were in cars are now farther away from the school than the bikers or walkers, that the bikers are farther away than the walkers, and that the walkers are still relatively close to the building. In a photo taken five minutes later, the people who were moving fastest would be even farther from the building. If you had several photos like this, you could trace back the motion of everybody and conclude that everyone left the building at the same moment in time.

In a way, the event that gave birth to the universe can be compared to this scene. At one point, all matter and energy was compressed into a very small space. Then, at a precise moment, in an incredible explosion, everything left. One big difference between school letting out and the beginning of the universe is that school lets the students out into streets that are already there—while the event that started the universe also *made the space* that the universe is in.

The stars in the universe are organized into giant groups called galaxies. By measuring the position of the galaxies in the universe today and the distances between them, scientists can calculate when all of the galaxies must have been together. They conclude that at a precise moment, about 14 billion years ago, all the matter that developed into our universe exploded in the most extreme burst of energy imaginable. It was in that moment, which scientists call the Big Bang, that the universe was born.

Cluster of galaxies

Clumps of hot blue stars began to form after the Big Bang.

# The Big Bang

How did the **universe** begin? It all started with the **Big Bang**, an unimaginably intense explosion that gave birth to all the space, matter, and energy that exist today. In other words, everything in the universe, from stars to planets to you, is made of the stuff that resulted from this event. The blast also produced energy, in the form of light and other waves that still echo today.

## Where did the Big Bang happen?

There is no special place in the universe that future tourists might visit to see the spot where the universe began. That's because the Big Bang was not an explosion *in* space but an explosion *of* space. So it happened *everywhere in the universe*, in all of space, including the space now taken up by your body! If you're finding this hard to imagine, you're not alone! The idea *is* difficult to grasp. But as you read this book and maybe others about astronomy, you'll find the idea makes more and more sense.

## What was it like right after the Big Bang?

In the moments after the Big Bang, the universe was unbelievably hot. After about three minutes, it had "cooled down" to a temperature of more than a *billion* degrees, about 70 times hotter than the center of the Sun. Nothing could survive in that heat. Life could not begin in the universe until everything had cooled off.

## How did the universe cool down?

Imagine a pot of water boiling on a stove. What happens to the steam when someone takes the lid off the pot? It expands and rushes out into the space around the pot, cooling down as it spreads out. The more the steam expands, the cooler it gets. The same thing happened to the universe. As space stretched, it cooled down. Today, space is very, very cold, because it has stretched so much. Only the stars, which make their own energy, and the planets that are close enough to stars to absorb their heat are hot now. The rest of the universe is icy cold.

BANG! BANG! BANG! BANG!

## NEWS FLASH!

Helium—the lighter-than-air gas that keeps balloons from falling to the ground—is a leftover of the Big Bang. During the initial explosion, the universe behaved like the superhot core of a star, turning hydrogen atoms into slightly more complex helium atoms. As the universe expanded and cooled, the extra helium gas created by the explosion remained.

This painting shows what the universe might have looked like about a billion years after the Big Bang, when many new stars were forming.

# How do we know the Big Bang really happened?

One of the best proofs of the Big Bang was found by accident in the 1960s. Two American scientists, Arno Penzias and Robert Wilson, were working for AT&T, a telephone company. They were trying to figure out how to use satellites in space to transmit long-distance phone calls. The company wanted to convert the sounds of the calls to radio waves and bounce them off orbiting satellites to come back to some other part of Earth. And they wanted the calls to stay clear, without any random noise, or static, from space getting into the conversation.

Penzias and Wilson were asked to check out where in space there might be annoying static, so that AT&T could place their satellites out of the way. To their amazement, the scientists discovered a faint kind of static coming from *everywhere* in the universe. No one before had ever discovered anything that came evenly from all directions at once. Soon, the scientists realized that they had actually tuned in on the leftover "flash" of a cosmic explosion that had to have filled *all of space at once*. This could only be the original blast—the Big Bang—that started the universe. As the universe cooled down, the light energy from this flash faded, but it didn't disappear. It lived on in the form of the radio-wave static detected by Penzias and Wilson. In 1978, the two scientists won the Nobel Prize in physics, the highest honor in science, for giving direct proof of the way the universe began.

New telescopes in space continue to explore the details of this leftover flash so we can learn more about the Big Bang.

*The Wilkinson MAP Satellite is one of the telescopes in space that is observing the details of the flash of the Big Bang. It is named after David Wilkinson, one of the scientists who first helped us understand the flash.*

# Galaxies:
## Islands in Space

Stars do not live alone. Just as people tend to gather in towns and cities, stars gather in giant groupings that astronomers call **galaxies**. Typical galaxies might have billions of stars in them. Each galaxy is like an island, surrounded by a sea of space. All the groups of galaxies together and the space between them make up what astronomers call the universe—everything that exists, from the tiniest speck of dust, to giant stars, to you!

▲ Galaxy M74 resembles our own galaxy, the Milky Way.

### Are all galaxies alike?

No. Galaxies come in many shapes and sizes. Some galaxies are heavily populated, containing billions of stars, while others have just a few million stars. Some are round like a blimp, while others are flat like a pancake. Some don't have any regular shape. These odd-shaped galaxies may have been disturbed by collisions with other galaxies over the huge stretch of cosmic history.

### Besides stars, what else is in a galaxy?

Galaxies also contain planets and moons, as well as chunks of rocks and ice called asteroids and comets. All galaxies also contain the raw material for making new stars and planets. This raw material is in the form of giant clouds of gas and dust.

WE LIVE ON AN ISLAND, TOO!

## NEWS FLASH!

- There are more stars in all the galaxies we can see than there are grains of sand on all the beaches of the world.

- The farthest galaxy we have discovered is so far away that light from it takes more than 12 billion years to reach us. The light we see tonight from that galaxy left on its journey to us long before the Sun and Earth ever existed.

### How many galaxies are in the universe?

There are hundreds of billions of galaxies out there, each with millions or billions of stars. And just as stars gather together in galaxies, galaxies gather together in groups, which you'll read about later in this chapter. Vast stretches of nearly empty space separate the galaxies.

### Do galaxies have names?

A few do, but there are too many galaxies to give them all names. Earth's home galaxy is called the Milky Way because its stars look like spilled milk across our sky. Some other galaxies have nicknames, too. The Andromeda Galaxy is named after the star pattern in which it is found. The Sombrero Galaxy got its name because astronomers thought it looked like a hat.

▲ The Andromeda Galaxy is the closest large galaxy to us.

## How do astronomers keep track of all the galaxies?

Astronomers record galaxies in catalogs. Today, the catalogs are kept on computers and are easily found on the Internet. Many new catalogs were compiled in the twentieth century. One earlier catalog was created by Charles Messier, a comet hunter, who, in 1781 made a list of all the bright, fuzzy space objects that were *not* comets. The objects he cataloged contain the prefix M and a number. Other astronomers created the New General Catalog, which they completed in 1888. Galaxies listed in this catalog contain the prefix NGC and a number. Some galaxies are listed in both of these catalogs and so have two different letter and number designations. The Andromeda Galaxy, for example, is called M31 in one catalog and NGC 224 in the other.

▼ The Sombrero Galaxy is a spiral galaxy with a thick core of stars.

## Distances in Space

Many objects in space, such as the Moon and some other planets in our solar system, are relatively close to Earth. We can see them without telescopes and can record their distance from us using common measurements like miles or kilometers.

Other things, like distant stars or the edge of our galaxy, are so far away that it's not practical to use miles or kilometers to measure their distances. Instead, astronomers use a unit called a light-year to measure the vastness of space. How far is that? A light-year is the distance that light travels in one year. Since light travels at about 670 million miles per hour (1.1 billion km/h)—faster than anything else in the universe—we can calculate that in a year, light travels about 6,000 billion miles (10,000 billion km). So, something that is one light year away is about 6,000 billion miles away.

Here's something else about space distances that's really amazing: The farther away something is, the further back in time its light began its journey. The light from the Sun, for instance, takes eight minutes to travel to Earth. So when we see its light, we're really seeing what the Sun looked like eight minutes ago. When astronomers look at things that are 2 million *light-years* away, such as the Andromeda Galaxy, they're seeing the light that left the galaxy 2 million years ago!

# A Cosmic Photo Album

The great astronomer Edwin Hubble was the first to prove—in the 1920s—that there were other galaxies out there, besides our own. He eventually described four different types of galaxies, based on their shapes—**spiral, barred spiral, elliptical** and **irregular**. The Hubble Space Telescope, which is named for Edwin Hubble, has taken some of the best pictures we've ever seen of distant galaxies.

## Is the Sun on one of the main spiral swirls of the Milky Way?

No. Our solar system is on a little side stream of stars, not on one of the main spiral swirls.

## What do the shape names mean?

A spiral galaxy is made of stars and dust that form a swirl around a bulge of stars in the middle of the galaxy. A barred-spiral galaxy has a bar of stars across its middle. An elliptical galaxy is round or blimp-shaped. An irregular galaxy is any shape that is difficult to describe. Our galaxy, the Milky Way, is a slightly barred spiral galaxy.

SMILE!

▲ *NGC 1350 is a spiral galaxy.*

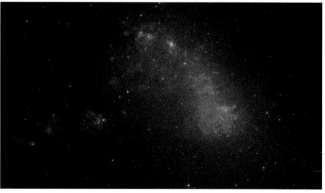

▲ *NGC 1300 is a barred-spiral galaxy.*

▲ *M60 (at left) is a giant elliptical galaxy.*

▲ *The Small Magellanic Cloud is an irregular galaxy.*

NGC 4414 is a spiral galaxy showing
lots of dust among its stars.

# The Milky Way Galaxy

Though the Milky Way is our home galaxy, it's actually harder for us to see than some distant galaxies. That's because we are *inside* it. Taking a picture of it is like trying to take a picture of yourself from inside your kneecap. You wouldn't get the clearest view from there! The Milky Way measures about 100,000 light-years across. Because Earth is more than 20,000 light-years from the outer edge of the Galaxy, it's impossible for us to travel outside of it to get a complete view.

The inner 900 light-years of our galaxy

## How can we learn about the Milky Way from inside it?

By looking carefully for stars and groups of stars that we can use as "signposts," scientists have learned quite a bit about the Milky Way. They can understand it even better by comparing it to other galaxies that look like it. Astronomers know, for instance, that it's a spiral galaxy, with billions of stars traveling in a giant disk around its center.

THE BEST THING ABOUT THE MILKY WAY IS ICE-CREAM!

## What's in the center of the Milky Way?

At the heart of our galaxy is a giant ball of collapsed material called a black hole. This black hole contains enough material to make more than 3 million suns! Astronomers know that this is a huge black hole because they observe stars whirling at great speeds around a seemingly empty space. The incredibly intense gravity of the black hole causes this. Surrounding the outer region of the black hole is a ball of stars about 12,000 light-years across.

### NEWS FLASH!

To count all 200 billion or so stars in the Milky Way Galaxy would take an amazing 1,268 years! And that's if you took only 5 seconds to say the average number, and you didn't stop to eat, sleep, or do anything else!

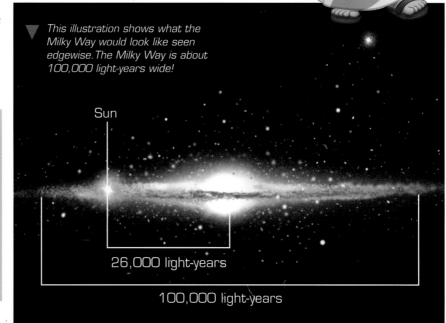

This illustration shows what the Milky Way would look like seen edgewise. The Milky Way is about 100,000 light-years wide!

Sun

26,000 light-years

100,000 light-years

This painting shows what the Milky Way might look like if we could see it from above.

## Can we see the center and other side of the Galaxy?

THERE'S DUST INSIDE THE MILKY WAY? THEY SHOULD SEE UNDER LILO'S BED!

Unfortunately, the view through our galaxy is not very clear. The dust inside the Milky Way builds up so that scientists cannot see light past 10,000 light-years or so from Earth. But astronomers have been able to collect radio waves and heat rays that go through dust to draw a good map of the other side of the Galaxy.

## Where is our solar system in the Milky Way?

The Sun and all the planets in our solar system are about 26,000 light-years from the center of the Milky Way. If you consider the ball of stars in the middle of the Milky Way to be the "city center" of the Galaxy, then you could say that our solar system is in the suburbs.

## Does our solar system move inside the Galaxy?

Yes! All the stars in a galaxy go around the center of the galaxy, and our Sun is no different! So while the planets are orbiting it, the Sun and everything else in our solar system is traveling around the center of the Milky Way. The journey takes about 225 million years for one trip. That means our solar system has traveled around the center of the Milky Way more than 20 times in the 4.6 billion years since the solar system formed.

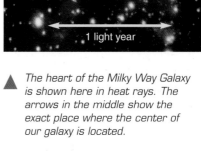

1 light year

The heart of the Milky Way Galaxy is shown here in heat rays. The arrows in the middle show the exact place where the center of our galaxy is located.

# The Local Group

The Milky Way Galaxy is part of a small group of galaxies that astronomers call the **Local Group**. That may not be a very original name, but it's a good way to describe cosmic neighbors. And just as everything in our solar system is always on the move around the Sun, all the galaxies in the Local Group swirl around the middle of the group.

## How many galaxies are in the Local Group?

Astronomers have found about 40 members so far, including three big spirals, two medium-sized ellipticals, and many smaller ellipticals and irregulars. However, astronomers are still finding new galaxies that are part of the Local Group.

SEE STITCH, WE WERE NEIGHBORS LONG BEFORE WE MET AND BECAME FAMILY!

◄ The faint fuzzy blob in this picture is a small elliptical galaxy in our Local Group. We see it through the many stars in our own Galaxy.

## NEWS FLASH!

The Milky Way is on a collision course with other galaxies! The newly discovered Canis Major Dwarf Galaxy, the Sagittarius Dwarf Galaxy, and other smaller galaxies will smash into our galaxy in the future. And the huge Andromeda Galaxy—it's headed our way, too. No need to worry, however. It will take more than 3 *billion* years to make contact.

## Why are scientists still finding new members of the Local Group?

The easiest galaxies to spot are the big, bright ones. It's similar to looking at city lights from a high-flying airplane at night. The lights of the big cities are easy to see. But from high up, the lights of the small towns are harder to spot, so we might miss them as we scan the landscape. Astronomers missed many tiny, faint galaxies until better telescopes were developed. Scientists now realize that there might be many more small, dim galaxies out there than they had been able to spot just a few years ago.

Besides Andromeda, M33 is the other big spiral galaxy in the Local Group.

## What galaxies are our closest neighbors?

The closest galaxy found so far is a tiny elliptical galaxy that astronomers call the Sagittarius Dwarf. It is only about 80,000 light-years away—which is a big distance compared to trips we take on Earth but a very small distance on the scale of galaxies. There may also be a broken-up galaxy only 25,000 light-years away, called the Canis Major Dwarf. This faint group of stars was discovered in 2003. It's still being studied by astronomers to see if it really should be classified as a galaxy.

## What is the biggest galaxy in the Local Group?

The biggest local galaxy is the Andromeda Galaxy. It is a beautiful spiral galaxy, wider than the Milky Way and with more material in it. It is located about 2 million light-years away from us. The Milky Way is the second-largest galaxy in the Local Group.

The Large Magellanic Cloud is an irregular galaxy that orbits the Milky Way. It's about 160,000 light-years away.

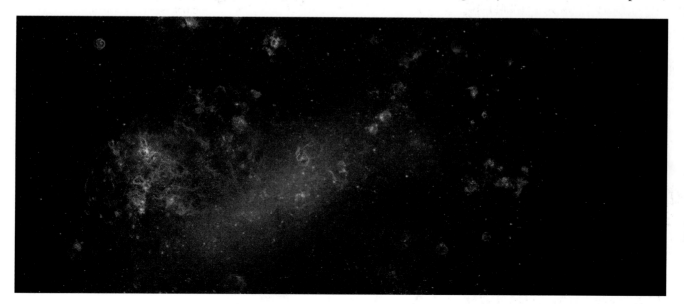

# Galaxy Clusters: The "Swiss Cheese" Universe

Sometimes groups of thousands of galaxies travel together through space in giant **galaxy clusters**. Other collections of galaxies, like our Local Group, contain just a small number of galaxies. And one of the most interesting discoveries astronomers have made is that the groups and clusters of galaxies also gather together into enormous **superclusters** that can stretch across the vastness of space for hundreds of millions of light-years.

## How does the universe look like Swiss cheese?

Good Swiss cheese has big holes in it, around which the cheese can be found. In the same way, astronomers are seeing that superclusters of galaxies are arranged around emptier regions, which they call **voids**. There are very few galaxies inside the voids but lots of them in the areas around the voids.

## What holds galaxy clusters and superclusters together?

The "cosmic glue" that holds these groups together is gravity. It is gravity that holds the moving planets to the Sun and doesn't let them fly into deep space. Gravity holds the moving stars within the Milky Way Galaxy and doesn't let them escape. And it is gravity, acting over huge distances, that keeps the galaxies in a cluster of galaxies in orbit around their common center.

## What is the closest cluster of galaxies?

The closest grouping of galaxies outside of the Local Group is called the Virgo Cluster, named after the constellation in which it is seen. The Virgo Cluster has thousands of member galaxies, many of which are very faint and hard to see. The center of this cluster is about 50 million light-years from Earth.

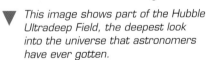

I CAN MAKE ANYTHING LOOK LIKE SWISS CHEESE!

▼ This image shows part of the Hubble Ultradeep Field, the deepest look into the universe that astronomers have ever gotten.

## NEWS FLASH!

Between September 2003 and January 2004, the Hubble Space Telescope spent 400 of its orbits around the Earth taking pictures of the same little dark spot in the sky. By adding all the pictures together on a computer, astronomers managed to get the deepest look ever into the universe. They estimate that the picture shows more than 10,000 galaxies in this one tiny spot.

Stephan's Quintet is a set of galaxies in a cluster interacting with each other and changing each other's shapes.

## Is our Local Group part of a supercluster?

Our Local Group and dozens of other groups and clusters of galaxies are all part of a huge supercluster called the Virgo Supercluster. It's called the Virgo Supercluster because the Virgo Cluster is in the middle of it. This supercluster is about 130 million light-years across.

## What do astronomers see beyond our supercluster?

Looking farther and farther into space, astronomers have made maps of thousands and thousands of galaxies beyond our own. These maps have allowed them to see how the universe is organized. It was by looking at the pattern of superclusters around the universe, that astronomers discovered the Swiss-cheese design.

I THINK MACADAMIA NUT CLUSTERS ARE PRETTY SUPER!

This group of galaxies is at the center of a cluster in the constellation of Norma.

# Galaxy Collisions and Mergers

Because galaxies are big and live in groups, they can crash into one another. If two galaxies of about the same size collide, astronomers call it a merger. But if a big galaxy pulls in a smaller one, it's more like a meal than a merger. Astronomers think that many of today's big galaxies grew by making meals of their smaller neighbors. Even our own Milky Way probably grew to its present size by swallowing smaller galaxies.

## What happens when two galaxies collide?

Galaxies contain not only stars but lots of raw material. The raw material is gas and dust that collects in huge clouds. When two giant clouds of gas and dust from different galaxies meet, they attract each other by mutual gravity. As the material in the clouds gets more concentrated, gravity can pull the dust and gas together until they start to make new stars. So when two large galaxies collide, we often see a burst of new stars being born, right where the raw material is thickest. Astronomers call such galaxies **starburst galaxies**. Also, after the collision, the new merged galaxy can take on a very unusual shape.

THAT'S MY KIND OF DIET!

### NEWS FLASH!

When galaxies were first discovered, astronomers thought that they were like islands in space which never came in contact with one another. But today, astronomers know that galaxies are more like bumper cars in an amusement park. They collide and sometimes stick together in bigger and bigger clumps. Many of the big galaxies we see probably grew from the collisions of many little ones.

## How does a larger galaxy "eat" a smaller one?

The gravity of the big galaxy pulls apart, or digests, the smaller one. Its stars become part of the star patterns in the big galaxy. Over millions of years, no real trace of the small victim galaxy might remain. Even after such a meal, the shape of the big galaxy may not change much. Astronomers think it takes many meals to make a galaxy grow.

## Can stars hit one another when galaxies collide?

When galaxies collide, the stars from the two galaxies rarely hit each other because stars are so far apart from one another. In fact, stars from different galaxies pass each other without being affected.

▼ These colliding galaxies are nicknamed "The Mice."

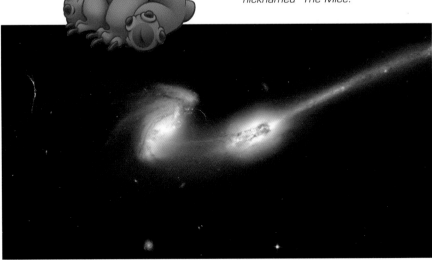

A smaller galaxy is being drawn into a larger one.

# Quasars:
## Tunnels to the Past

In the 1960s, astronomers discovered some dim celestial objects that, at first, they thought were stars. The astronomers soon found that, unlike stars, the objects were moving away from our galaxy at great speeds. They were also sending out strong radio waves. Stars send out few radio waves. Astronomers called the mysterious things "quasi-stellar radio sources," from the Latin words for "almost star." The name was soon shortened to **quasars**.

## What is a quasar?

It took about two decades of work by astronomers around the world to discover that quasars really are galaxies—with a surprise in the middle. The bright centers of these galaxies glow more intensely than all the faint stars around them. So, from far away, most of the galaxy is too dim to see, but the center looks like a shining star.

▲ This galaxy, M87, contains a black hole that has already eaten enough material to make more than two and a half billion Suns! You can see one of the jets of "spit out" material going off to the left.

### NEWS FLASH!

- The farthest quasars are so distant that we see them as they were 12 billion years ago or more.
- The most distant quasars are moving away from us at nearly the speed of light.

I GOT QUEASY ON A QUASAR ONCE.

## What makes quasars appear so bright?

The brightness actually comes from stars, gas clouds, and dust falling into overfed black holes! In the centers of galaxies, stars and gas are very crowded. If one star collapses and turns into a black hole, it will have a lot of "food" in the neighborhood to eat. Over millions of years, a black hole at the center of a galaxy will swallow many stars and much gas and dust and will grow to be a much bigger black hole. Its increased gravity will pull even more stuff toward it. Sometimes a small galaxy will collide with a larger galaxy that contains a giant black hole at its center. A whole galaxy is too much for a black hole to eat all at once because the "mouth" of any black hole is tiny. So, if too much material from the colliding galaxy starts to enter the black hole, some of the material will actually be "spit out" before it is swallowed. This rejected material generally forms two great jets of outgoing material as it blasts back into space.

This galaxy is nicknamed the "Egg Yolk Galaxy." It has a brilliant center where a hungry black hole is overeating.

FEEDING STITCH IS LIKE FEEDING A BLACK HOLE!

## Can things fall out of a black hole?

Once anything reaches the edge of a black hole, it is trapped and cannot get out. But if the material is swirled away *before* it reaches the mouth of the black hole, it can be thrown outward with great force. The material being whirled away will light up with lots of energy, making the neighborhood of the big black hole very bright.

## Why are there more quasars far away from Earth?

When astronomers look far out into space, they are seeing back in time. Light takes time to reach us, so when scientists see a quasar 10 billion light-years away, they see it the way it was 10 billion years ago. Remember: a quasar black hole "lights up" when there is too much "food" coming in. There were more collisions of galaxies early in the history of the universe than there are today. So there was more food available to feed black holes back then. In a way, quasars are like time tunnels, letting astronomers look back to the early days of the universe, when overfed black holes were more common.

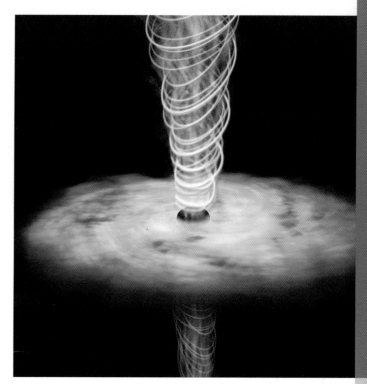

This painting shows what a black hole inside a quasar galaxy might look like.

# The Expanding Universe

In the 1920s, Edwin Hubble used the world's largest telescope to measure the movement of galaxies and their distance from one another. First, he looked at the Local Group of galaxies. These galaxies, he found, travel together, circling around the center of the group. But, when Hubble looked outside the Local Group, he was very surprised. Every galaxy he found outside the Local Group was moving away from our group of galaxies.

### What did Hubble's discovery mean?

Hubble—and other astro-nomers who have studied galaxies—realized that all other galaxies were not only moving away from us, they were moving away from each other. They realized that the whole universe was getting larger! This idea of the **expanding universe** is one of the most important discoveries in all of astronomy.

### Are all the galaxies moving away at the same speed?

No. Hubble found that the groups of galaxies are not moving at the same speed at all. The farther the cluster is from another cluster, the faster it moves away! All galaxies are moving away from us, except those in our Local Group. But closer galaxies move away from us more slowly. The distant galaxies move faster. This idea is called *Hubble's Law*.

### What makes the galaxies move?

Galaxies don't have any way of making themselves move. Instead, it is *space itself that is stretching*. Think of space as a balloon. When you blow up a balloon, where does new balloon skin come from? It comes from the stretching of the balloon skin you already have. In the same way, when space stretches, new space comes from the space that was already there. As space stretches, it carries the galaxies away from each other in all directions.

### Why is space stretching?

The universe began with a big stretch—the Big Bang. That stretching is still going on—all the result of that initial explosion.

### NEWS FLASH!

If you think that the expansion of the entire universe is really too mind-boggling, don't feel bad. Albert Einstein, one of the smartest people who ever lived, also had trouble with it. He made up a whole part of his theories just to explain how the universe wouldn't expand. Later he called it the biggest blunder of his life.

DON'T WORRY, STITCH. I'LL NEVER MOVE AWAY FROM YOU!

◀ *This photograph shows a rich cluster of galaxies. All of them participate in the expansion of the universe.*

*The Whirlpool Galaxy is interacting with a smaller neighbor. Both are about 25 million light-years from Earth.*

# Measuring Time:
## The Cosmic Year

In this make-believe year, we imagine that the Big Bang took place at the first moment of January 1. Today, as you are reading this book, it's exactly midnight on December 31. Between those two dates, everything else that happened in the universe fits in.

For example, astronomers estimate that the Milky Way formed in February of the cosmic year. Our solar system formed much later—somewhere around the beginning of September. Earth formed in late September, and life on Earth appeared by the end of September. The earliest forms of life all lived in the ocean; life on land did not appear until around December 20. By December 21, great forests began to grow on the land. The last dinosaurs roamed on December 30.

Hominids—the first humanlike mammals—first stepped foot into our world sometime after 9 p.m. on December 31, which, in real time, was about 4 million years ago. Humans created written language about 12 seconds before midnight on December 31.

Using the cosmic year as a analogy helps us see that humans have existed for a very, very short time in the history of the universe.

Big Bang

Our solar system forms

Human life begins

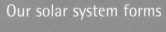

Today

Age of the dinosaurs

To help us understand spans of billions of years, astronomers have looked for ways to explain the long history of the universe. They know that people can easily imagine an Earth year—365 days, divided up into 12 months. So they said, "Let's pretend that the universe was just one Earth-year old." They called this explanation "the cosmic year."

January

February

Milky Way forms

March

April

May

June

July

August

Earth forms

September

Life on Earth begins

October

November

Life begins on land

December

# Exploration
# & Discovery

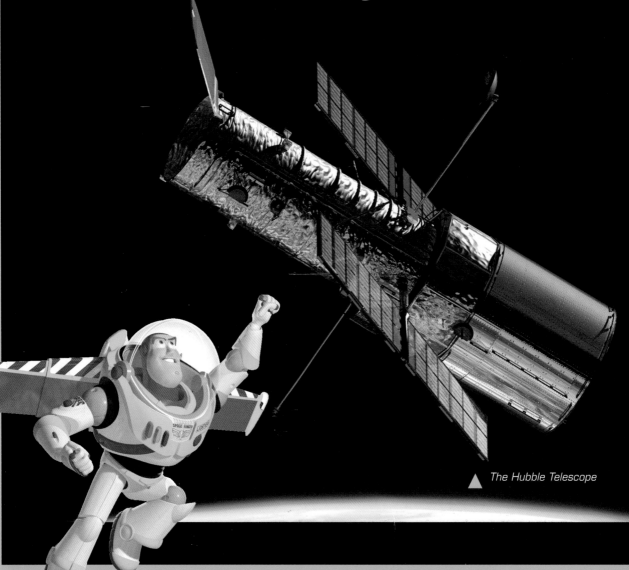

▲ The Hubble Telescope

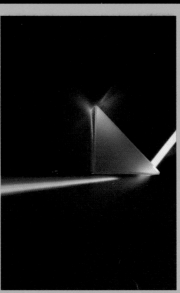

▲ Stonehenge                    ▲ Galileo telescope                    ▲ Light through a prism                    ▲ Astronaut on
                                                                                                              the Moon

For most of human history, astronomers had to depend upon their eyes alone to learn about the universe. By keeping track of the heavens, ancient astronomers could follow and predict the motions of the Sun, the Moon, and the planets in the sky. Early people learned to navigate by the stars, created calendars based on the phases of the Moon, and built monuments that tracked the yearly movements of the Sun. They did all this without the aid of modern tools, using only the light that the stars make and the planets reflect.

Curiosity, however, led astronomers to find a way of seeing more than their eyes alone could perceive. To understand more about what was out there, they needed some kind of tool to show parts of the universe hidden from our sight. The invention of the telescope in the early 1600s allowed astronomers to see farther into space. The telescope revealed things that were too dim for the human eye alone to see. Astronomers found a host of new things in the sky they had never

dreamed were there. At first, telescopes used lenses to collect more light. Later, astronomers substituted mirrors, which allowed them to build telescopes that capture even more light and see even deeper into the universe.

Starting in 1800, scientists discovered other, invisible, waves that could help them understand what was out there— radar and X-rays, for example. By the end of the twentieth century, they were able to put telescopes into space, send robot probes to the planets, and even send people into space. Humans took their first steps on another world in 1969, when astronauts first explored the Moon.

Today, at the dawn of the twenty-first century—your century—astronomers have robot rovers exploring Mars, a probe that landed on one of Saturn's moons, and telescopes in orbit taking pictures of distant places that have never been seen by human eyes. Who knows how far into the universe future technology will allow mankind to explore.

*Cassini Space Probe near Saturn*

*Galileo Space Probe*

# Early Astronomy

The sky you see is essentially the same one that ancient sky watchers admired. They saw the Sun appear to rise in the east and set in the west every day. They watched the Moon go through its monthly cycle—from the tiniest crescent to a full sphere and back again. The patterns among the stars fueled their imaginations. While records of much of their early work is lost, these astronomers left behind drawings and monuments that record a deep interest in the sky.

## Did ancient people think the world was flat?

Many did, but those who studied the skies were the first to learn the truth. By the fourth century B.C., Greek sky watchers knew that Earth was round by observing that it makes a round shadow on the Moon. Some even thought that the Earth traveled around the Sun, though at the time this idea seemed quite unbelievable. It wasn't until the seventeenth century that these facts became widely accepted.

### DID YOU KNOW?

In the year 1600, the Italian astronomer and philosopher Giordano Bruno was burned at the stake for suggesting that there might be planets around other stars with intelligent creatures on them. (Luckily, astronomers who think this way today are not treated quite so roughly.)

## Did all ancient cultures study astronomy?

The sky was important to all cultures in different ways. But only some ancient people left us their records. Early people in Europe, Asia, and Central America built amazing monuments that show their knowledge of the stars and planets. Chinese astronomers kept careful notes of lights that appeared in the sky, such as comets and exploding stars. Astronomers today can track sky history using the thousands of years of information in the records these skywatchers kept.

IT'S SCARY AND DARK IN ANDY'S ROOM WHEN THE MOON IS UP. I LIKE THE SUN BETTER!

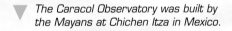
The Caracol Observatory was built by the Mayans at Chichen Itza in Mexico.

▲ Stonehenge helped ancient people keep track of the passing year and predict eclipses.

## What ancient astronomical monuments can still be seen today?

There are many examples. One is Stonehenge, built in England over a period of about 1,300 years, starting in 2800 B.C. This amazing group of stones was used to keep track of the passing of the year by pointing to the place where the Sun could be seen rising on the horizon. The arrangement of the stones along with additional markers could also predict important sky events, such as **eclipses**. The remains of the Caracol Observatory, built by the Mayans at Chichen Itza in Mexico starting around 1000 A.D., show this culture's deep interest in understanding the cycles of the sky. The ancient Egyptians used the stars to precisely line up some of the pyramids with north, south, east, and west.

## How did ancient people use their knowledge of the stars?

They navigated and kept track of time. Polynesian sailors used the stars to steer a course from one island to another for thousands of years before European sailors had this knowledge. As long ago as 4200 B.C., the ancient Egyptians knew that a year had 365 days. And the Mayans in Central America created a calendar based on the movement of Venus.

## Tycho Brahe's Great Observatory

For all of human history until the early 1600s, astronomers learned about the heavens just by using their eyes and minds. Astronomers eventually used instruments to measure the positions of the lights in the sky as accurately as possible. The last great astronomer to work without a telescope was the Danish nobleman Tycho Brahe, who persuaded the king of Denmark to build him a complicated **observatory** on an island off the coast of Denmark. With a device similar to a giant protractor, a tool that measures angles, Tycho was able to measure the motions of the planets more precisely than anyone before him had done.

▼ This picture shows the position of the morning Sun over the course of a full year above a temple at Delphi in Greece. The Sun's location in the morning sky changes continuously week to week.

# Telescopes

The history of astronomy changed forever when the telescope was invented in the early 1600s. Before that, astronomers only had their eyes with which to observe the sky. In the eye, the opening that lets light in is tiny—only about ¼ inch (0.6 cm) wide. That is fine for seeing bright sunlight, but it's too small for tracking dim stars or faraway planets. A telescope helps the human eye catch more of the light that has been made by stars or reflected by planets.

◄ This giant 200-inch reflector is on Mount Palomar in California.

## How does a telescope work?

In a telescope, specially shaped lenses or mirrors gather the light and focus it. Think of telescopes as buckets for light. Just as a bigger bucket can carry more water, the bigger the lens or mirror, the more light the telescope can collect. The more light the telescope gathers, the better it can reveal faint objects.

## DID YOU KNOW?

With the biggest telescopes, we can see galaxies 12 *billion* light-years away. These galaxies are so far away that the light we see tonight left these galaxies 12 billion years ago—nearly at the birth of the universe!

## What kinds of telescopes are there?

Telescopes that collect light with lenses are called **refractors**. Telescopes that use mirrors to gather more light are called **reflectors**. The biggest single mirrors made so far are part of the Large Binocular Telescope, near Safford, Arizona, and are 328 inches (840 cm) wide. In some telescopes, more than one mirror is used to collect more light. Some telescopes collect rays that are not visible to the eye. For example, some telescopes use big metal dishes to collect radio waves.

I THINK I'M PRETTY FOCUSED EVEN WITHOUT A TELESCOPE!

▼ The Very Large Telescope in Chile consists of four large reflectors.

Galileo's telescopes

The biggest refractor is at the Yerkes Observatory, outside of Chicago, Illinois. It has a lens 40 inches (16 cm) wide! The largest mirrored telescope in the world, in the Andes Mountains of Chile, is aptly named the Very Large Telescope. It's made of four mirrors set in four telescopes that are connected together to make a reflector about 640 inches (1,640 cm) across! High atop a volcanic peak in Hawaii are the two Keck telescopes. Each telescope uses a combination of 36 mirrors that together are 400 inches (1,025 cm) wide.

## Who was the first astronomer to use a telescope?

No one knows exactly who first had the idea of using a pair of eyeglass lenses set inside a tube to get a better look at the heavens, but the first person who took a look *and* kept careful records of what a telescope could reveal in the night sky was Galileo Galilei. His telescopes, tiny by today's standards, with lenses only one or two inches (2.5–5 cm) across, changed our view of the universe forever.

## What did Galileo discover with his telescopes?

In 1609, Galileo found four moons going around Jupiter and quickly understood that if moons could revolve around Jupiter, maybe Earth was not the center of everything, as most people then believed. Galileo also discovered that Earth's moon had mountains and valleys and was not as smooth as things in the heavens were thought to be. He also saw that the Milky Way and other fuzzy patches of the sky were actually made of many individual stars.

## Who built the first telescope that used mirrors?

The mirror pioneer was Isaac Newton, the great scientist who first explained the physics of motion and gravity. In 1671, Newton showed how to make a practical telescope using a mirror instead of a lens as the main light collector. Reflectors could be built much larger in diameter and could collect more light. By 1845, Lord Rosse in Ireland had built a reflector with a 72-inch (183-cm) mirror.

Newton's reflector telescope contains a mirror at the bottom of the tube.

# Visible & Invisible Waves

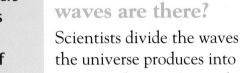

For a long time, the only waves from space that astronomers knew about were visible light waves. Until 1800, scientists didn't even know that other, invisible waves existed. But now we know that visible light is part of a whole family of waves called **electromagnetic radiation**. The microwaves that cook a snack are an example of such radiation. Microwaves are not visible to the eye. The X-rays your dentist uses are also part of this family of invisible waves.

## Why are light waves so useful to astronomers?

By studying light waves from stars, astronomers can learn how hot the stars are, what they are made of, and how they are moving. Light is a great messenger for telling astronomers about the universe. It travels at an amazing rate of 670 million miles per hour. Nothing in the universe travels faster!

### DID YOU KNOW?

- Sound does not travel in space because sound waves travel through air, and there's no air in space. So if you scream in space, no one will hear you.
- The light and other waves from the stars carry information "coded" into them about how hot the stars are and what they are made of.
- Astronomers have used microwave antennas to pick up the afterglow of the Big Bang, which is detected as microwaves from all directions in space.

## What kinds of light waves are there?

Scientists divide the waves the universe produces into six general categories: radio waves, infrared waves, visible light, ultraviolet waves, X-rays, and gamma rays. Radio waves and infrared waves are more stretched out than visible light; ultraviolet waves, X-rays, and gamma rays are less stretched out. Microwaves are a kind of radio wave, but these are shorter than the ones your car radio receives.

MY MIDDLE MAKES A WAVE WHEN I MOVE REAL SLOW!

## Why can't we see these other kinds of waves?

Our eyes evolved to see the kind of light that would help us survive. Here on Earth, the biggest source of light (and energy) is the Sun, so our eyes developed to see the peak of its light. There aren't a lot of X-rays on the Earth's surface, so eyes attuned to X-rays would have done little to help us survive.

## How do we find these waves if we can't see them with our eyes?

We use detectors: instruments that register these waves. For most of human history, the only light detector we had was our eyes. But then we invented photography. A new kind of detector, called film, could record what was in the sky. Today, film is being replaced by electronic detectors that turn each point of light into a tiny current of electricity. Then the amount of light in every part of a photo can be measured and recorded as a number, or digit. This is how digital photography works. Astronomers have developed special films and electronic detectors for recording invisible light, too.

1

*Visible light*

2

*Radio waves*

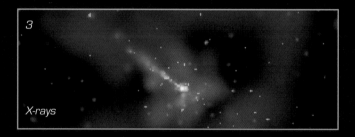

3

*X-rays*

4

*Infrared light*

## Four Views of the Same Galaxy

Things look different when seen with different waves. These four pictures all show Centaurus A, a large galaxy that "ate" a small neighbor about 100 million years ago. The center of Centaurus A is being "overfed," and great jets of glowing gas are coming out from the middle in opposite directions.

Picture 1 shows what the galaxy looks like with visible light. It has a belt of dust and newly born stars across its middle.

Picture 2 shows the galaxy as seen with radio waves. All you see are two jets coming out of the belt region.

Picture 3 shows the galaxy as seen in X-rays. You see presence of the overfed black hole as a point in the middle, one of the jets, and mysterious rings of hot glowing gas.

Picture 4 shows the two galaxies with infrared light. The leftover stuff from the victim galaxy can be seen as a red rectangle in the center.

IT'S MY DUTY TO BLOCK OUT ANY HARMFUL WAVES FROM ANDY'S ROOM!

## How do light waves move?

Unlike waves in the ocean, which move through water, or sound waves, which move through air, light waves don't need a medium through which to travel. In other words, *light moves itself*. This is why light (and the other members of its family of waves) can come to us through the emptiness of space.

## Do all the waves from space make it to Earth's surface?

No. Our planet's layers of air block many waves from reaching us. The high ozone layer in the atmosphere, for example, blocks most of the ultraviolet waves from ever getting to the surface. That's a good thing, because ultraviolet light can harm our skin and eyes. But this means that astronomers who want to study ultraviolet waves coming from space must put their instruments into space, beyond the ozone layer.

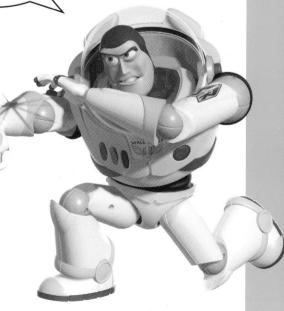

# Telescopes in Space

The atmosphere of Earth can be a real problem for astronomers. Of course, we need the air to breathe and the clouds to help circulate our water. But the clouds, the fog, the smog, and the smoke in our air can also stop starlight from coming to our eyes or from reaching our telescopes on Earth. And there are some kinds of waves—such as ultraviolet and X-rays—that are completely blocked by Earth's atmosphere.

## How can we see things in space that are blocked by the air?

If you want to see ultraviolet waves or X-rays from space, you have to go where there is no more air. Some of the most important telescopes astronomers use today orbit just above our planet's atmosphere. For example, NASA has been putting a series of observatories into orbit. These scan the sky using many different kinds of waves.

> I'LL FLY SO FAR INTO SPACE ONLY A TELESCOPE WILL FIND ME!

## DID YOU KNOW?

Since they can't be plugged in to an electrical outlet, space telescopes must make their own energy using solar panels. Energy from the Sun is captured with special cells that convert light into electricity. The electricity is stored in batteries for when it is needed. For example, the Hubble has six special batteries that can store as much energy as 20 car batteries.

## Who first had the idea that we could put telescopes in space?

In 1946, Lyman Spitzer, an astronomer who worked at Princeton University, first suggested that we could put a telescope in orbit to see the universe more clearly. This was a full decade before the first satellite was ever launched into space. One of the big telescopes orbiting Earth is now named in Spitzer's honor.

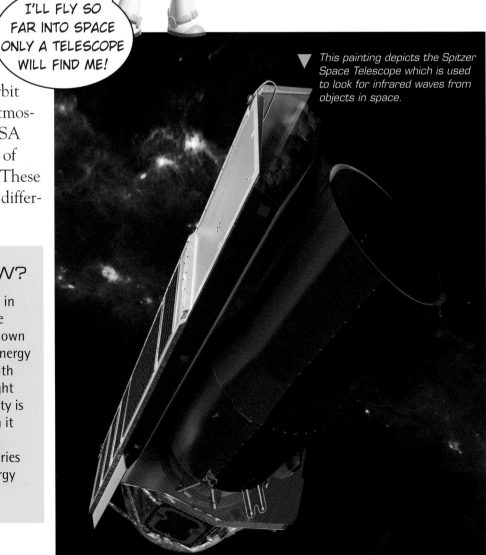

This painting depicts the Spitzer Space Telescope which is used to look for infrared waves from objects in space.

▲ This painting shows the Chandra Telescope which observes X-rays coming from space.

## What observatories are in space now?

The most famous is the Hubble Space Telescope, launched in 1990 and still going around Earth every 97 minutes. It can catch visible light, ultraviolet light, and infrared light. Astronauts have visited the Hubble four times to repair parts that were not working or to install better detectors and cameras on the telescope. The Chandra Observatory is used to scan the skies for X-rays. And the Spitzer Space Telescope searches out objects that glow with infrared waves. There are also many smaller telescopes in space, including several that are designed to search for great bursts of cosmic gamma rays.

*The Hubble Space Telescope in orbit above the Earth* ▶

## How does information from space telescopes get back to Earth?

All these telescopes gather a huge amount of information for astronomers every year. For example, the Hubble collects so many pictures and so much data that each day they would fill six computer CD-ROMs. All this information is converted to numbers and sent back to Earth using a radio antenna on the Hubble. The radio waves are gathered by NASA's big dish antennas and eventually sent to the Space Telescope Science Institute in Baltimore, Maryland. There, scientists use computers to translate some of the numbers back into pictures.

# Radio Telescopes

Radio waves from space make a hissing noise, called static, when they are translated into sound. In the early 1930s, a young engineer, Karl Jansky, discovered some static from outer space. Using an antenna, he found natural radio waves coming from the center of our Milky Way Galaxy. With this accidental discovery, the new field of radio astronomy began. Today, all over the world, big **radio telescopes**—often called "dishes"—catch radio waves from space.

## What are radio waves?

The term "radio wave" can be confusing. The waves that you hear from your radio at home or in the car are *sound waves* made by the speaker in the radio. **Radio waves** are the invisible waves that travel between the radio source—such as your favorite station—and the radio receiver—such as the radio in your car. Radio waves travel at the speed of light and can go through solid materials. Radio waves also bring calls to cell phones. These waves are members of the family of electromagnetic waves, along with light, X-rays, and infrared waves.

TO HEAR ME, ALL ANDY NEEDS TO DO IS PULL MY STRING!

## DID YOU KNOW?

The bowl-shaped dish of the Arecibo radio telescope is so large that it could hold 353 million family-sized boxes of cornflakes!

## What makes radio waves in space?

Many objects in the sky give off radio static. Huge cold clouds of gas in deep space make faint radio waves that come from the vibration of the many atoms of hydrogen they contain. These radio waves have shown astronomers that there are a lot of loose atoms between the stars. Other sources of cosmic radio waves are the "corpses" of exploded stars. Radio waves from such corpses allow astronomers to find the places where big stars have ended their lives. Two galaxies that collide can produce radio waves, too.

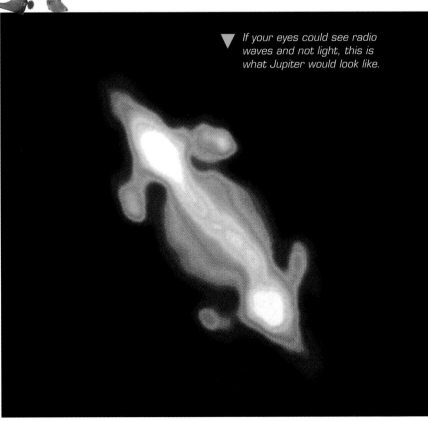

▼ *If your eyes could see radio waves and not light, this is what Jupiter would look like.*

The Very Large Array of radio dishes is on the Plains of San Agustin, New Mexico.

## Where is the biggest radio telescope in the world?

The biggest radio dish is in Puerto Rico. Engineers covered an entire valley with reflecting metal, making a dish 1,000 feet (305 meters) in diameter, and 167 feet (51 meters) deep. From three huge towers, on the hilltops above the dish, cables are strung for holding the antennas that catch the focused radio waves. The big dish can also be used as a radar reflector and send radar beams to bounce off the planets.

## What other kinds of telescopes do scientists use to capture radio waves?

Astronomers can connect many smaller radio dishes together, into what they call a **radio array**. The Very Large Array in New Mexico, for example, consists of 27 radio dishes, each 82 feet (25 meters) wide.

OH! SCIENTISTS CAPTURE RADIO WAVES LIKE THE CLAW CAPTURES US!

The largest radio dish in the world can be found at the Arecibo Observatory in Puerto Rico.

# Space Travelers

The Space Age began in 1957 when Russian engineers launched *Sputnik 1*, the first object built by humans to go into space. Scientists and engineers have been busy ever since, launching three kinds of spacecraft: **Earth satellites**, machines that orbit our planet; **planetary probes**, machines that fly by or orbit other worlds; and **spaceships**, which carry human passengers.

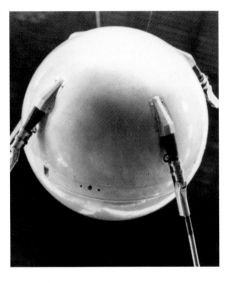

Sputnik 1 *was the first human-made object to leave Earth's atmosphere.*

## What was the first probe to escape Earth's gravity?

On January 2, 1959, the Russian-launched probe *Luna 1* flew by the Moon after 34 hours of flight. A year and a half earlier *Sputnik 1* had orbited Earth but had not escaped our planet's gravity.

## DID YOU KNOW?

- The oldest person to go into space was John Glenn, who flew aboard the space shuttle in 1998 at age 77.
- The longest space walks were taken by Jim Voss and Susan Helms on March 11, 2001. They spent 8 hours and 56 minutes outside the International Space Station.
- The person who spent the most time in space was Sergei Krikalev, who accumulated 803 days, 9 hours, and 39 minutes in space over the course of six different missions.

## Who was the first human being to go into outer space?

Yuri Gagarin of Russia was the first person to reach space, on April 12, 1961, in a tiny spaceship called *Vostok (East) 1*. He spent one hour and 48 minutes in space and became an instant hero around the world. The first woman to go into space was Valentina Tereshkova in June 1963.

TO INFINITY AND BEYOND!

## Who was first person to take a walk in space?

Alexei Leonov of Russia was the first human to go outside a spacecraft in a spacesuit, during the *Voskhod 2* mission in March 1965. In the 12 minutes outside his craft, Leonov's spacesuit got bigger and bigger because the air inside it had expanded in the airlessness of space! When he got back to the entrance to his spacecraft, he couldn't fit through the opening! Leonov had to slowly let air out of his suit so he could reenter. He was attached to the spaceship by a tether with which he could pull himself back. The first astronaut to let go of the tether was Bruce McCandless in February 1984. He was wearing a rocket pack on his back called the Manned Maneuvering Unit, which let him jet back to the space shuttle when he completed his space walk.

## Who was the first person to set foot on another world?

Neil Armstrong of the United States first stepped onto the surface of the Moon on July 21, 1969. As he stepped down, he said, "That's one small step for a man, one giant leap for mankind."

◀ *Neil Armstrong (left) and Buzz Aldrin on the Moon*

## Are astronauts "weightless" in space?

Some people think that astronauts are so far from Earth, they don't feel its gravity. But manned spacecraft fly only a few hundred miles above Earth, where gravity is still quite strong, and anyone or anything not moving would fall to the ground. The real story is that spaceships are moving so fast that they fall *around* the Earth instead of *to* the Earth. When an orbiting shuttle falls around Earth, everything inside it falls at the same rate. This means people and pencils and sandwiches all fall together with the ship, which makes everything and everyone seem "weightless."

▲ *Astronauts Lisa M. Nowak, Michael E. Fossum, and Stephanie D. Wilson aboard the Space Shuttle Discovery in 2006.*

## Where Does Space Begin?

Earth's atmosphere doesn't have a sharp edge to it. It just gets thinner the farther from the surface you travel. Still, scientists have now measured that 99.99 percent of our air is within 60 miles (97 km) of the surface. So 60 miles above the surface of Earth is a good place to think of as beginning of space. That might not seem so high until you compare it to other heights. For example, Earth's tallest mountain is about 5½ miles (9km) high. Jet planes travel at about 5 to 7½ miles (8 to12 km) above Earth.

▼ *Earth*

## Will space travel become common?

To get into space, you need to travel at about 17,000 miles per hour (28,000 kilometers per hour). And you need a powerful rocket to get you going that fast. High-speed rockets (and capsules to protect you once you are in space) are not cheap. So scientists don't think many people will be going into space anytime soon.

# Robot Probes & Landers

Sky watchers are no longer stuck studying the planets from Earth. We now have the tools to see other planets and moons up close. At first, our probes just flew by a planet or two. Later, other probes went into orbit around various planets, and astronomers could see the same sights over and over, giving them a fuller picture of a planet's atmosphere and surface. A few probes have even landed on other worlds and sent back information from the surface.

## What have orbiting probes accomplished?

The *Magellan* spacecraft, using radar to capture images, orbited Venus from 1990 to 1994, giving astronomers the first look through its thick clouds. Between 1995 and 2003, the *Galileo* craft made 34 orbits through the Jupiter system, giving us fabulous pictures of both the planet and its four large moons. Several probes are orbiting Mars right now and showing us amazing details of the surface of the red planet. And, since 2004, the *Cassini* spacecraft has been flying through the Saturn system, revealing secrets of the planet's rings and moons.

## On what worlds have probes landed?

Robot spacecraft have now landed on the Moon, Venus, Mars, one comet, and two asteroids. Three robot rovers, named *Sojourner*, *Spirit*, and *Opportunity*, have driven on the red sands of Mars. But the most exciting landing happened in January 2005, when the *Huygens* spacecraft touched down on the surface of Titan, Saturn's big moon. The probe took pictures and found "rocks" of ice and river channels carrying liquid methane.

▼ A painting of the Galileo *spacecraft receiving some data (the blue dots) from the probe it dropped into the atmosphere of Jupiter*

## DID YOU KNOW?

**Space Firsts:**

- The first flyby of another planet took place on December 14, 1962, when *Mariner 2* flew by Venus.

- The first landing on the Moon happened on January 31, 1966, when *Luna 9* landed without crashing.

- The first landing on another planet occurred on December 15, 1970, when *Venera 7* landed on Venus.

- The first flyby of an asteroid was on October 29, 1991, when the *Galileo* spacecraft traveled within 1,000 miles (1,600 kilometers) of the asteroid Gaspra.

An artist shows what the Huygens lander looked like on the surface of Saturn's moon Titan. The strings lead to the parachute that helped the probe land.

## Has a probe ever crashed into a planet?

Yes! In 2003, the *Galileo* probe dived into Jupiter at over 100,000 miles per hour (160,000 km per hour). Since Jupiter has no solid surface, it was like plunging into an ocean. Once its parachute and Jupiter's air slowed it down, the Galileo probe fell another 120 miles (193 km) before burning up, and sent back precious information about what the layers of Jupiter are like.

## Probing Beyond Pluto

Five spacecraft are leaving our solar system forever: two *Pioneers*, two *Voyagers*, and the *New Horizons* probe launched toward Pluto in 2006. They are the first objects made by humans to go into deep space. The first four of these probes have messages onboard in case someone or something finds them out there in the distant future and wonders who sent them. The two *Voyagers*, for example, have an audio and video disk with the sights and sounds of Earth. There are pictures from around the planet, natural sounds, and music from many countries. Even if any beings who might find the disk don't know how to play it, they will probably conclude that some type of intelligent life made the spacecraft on which it's flying.

OUR MISSION: PROBE ANDY'S ROOM!

This painting shows the Cassini spacecraft orbiting near Saturn.

91

# The Search for Intelligent Life

What's the most exciting astronomy project one can imagine? It could be finding new planets, looking back to the Big Bang, or searching for black holes. Many people would pick the search for signals from intelligent beings on another planet. Scientists can define an intelligent civilization as one that has an interest in astronomy. Really! If aliens out there don't have an interest in astronomy, they wouldn't think about communicating with other planets.

## Have alien spaceships landed on Earth?

Lots of movies and TV shows have suggested that spaceships from other worlds have landed or crashed on Earth. But scientists need *evidence*—proof—before they accept any claims like that. So far, there is simply no evidence that alien ships have been here.

*I CAN HELP YOU LOOK FOR INTELLIGENT LIFE!*

## How can we get in touch with aliens?

There are lots of ways we might get a message or send one all the way to the stars. For example, we might build a giant flashlight to signal that we are here. But there is already a blindingly bright source of light close to the Earth—the Sun. So scientists might prefer to use a messenger that doesn't have so much competition. It should also be a message that's easy to send. For these reasons, astronomers have decided that radio waves are the best messengers. We already use radio to send long-distance messages on Earth, so we have a lot of experience with them.

### DID YOU KNOW?

Several scientific groups, including the SETI Institute, have programs to try to find some kind of intelligent radio message. A new project, now being built in northern California, called the Allen Telescope Array, will search 100,000 stars to see if anyone out there might be sending out a message we can "overhear."

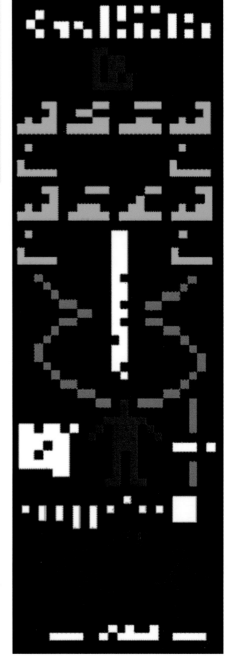

▲ This is a rough example of the kind of message astronomers think civilizations might exchange. A radio telescope is shown in purple at the bottom. Above it is a diagram of the Sun and its planets. The red figure above that represents human beings. This message was actually sent to the stars in 1974 from the Arecibo radio observatory by astronomer Frank Drake of the SETI Institute.

**Since we wouldn't speak the same language as the aliens, how could we understand each other?**

Astronomers plan to use pictures and diagrams to communicate with other civilizations. A scientific organization called the SETI Institute is coming up with all kinds of ideas for messages we could use without knowing the other's language. (SETI stands for Search for Extraterrestrial Intelligence.) One idea would be to send TV pictures, without sound.

WE CAN COMMUNICATE WITH THE OUTSIDE.

## Making Contact

The very first project to search for radio messages from civilizations among the stars began in 1960 and was called Project Ozma, after the princess in the books about the land of Oz by L. Frank Baum. Astronomer Frank Drake, who ran that project, thought that the land of Oz was a great fictional example of another world with unusual creatures.

In 1974, astronomers used the giant Arecibo radio dish in Puerto Rico to send humanity's first intentional message to possible alien civilizations. It was aimed at a cluster of about 300,000 stars 21,000 light-years away. It will be at least 42,000 years before we can hope to get an answer!

What happens if astronomers find a message? The first thing scientists will do is check to see if other telescopes besides the one that discovered the message are receiving it, too. This helps guard against hackers and practical jokers. Once they are sure, astronomers will release the message like any other scientific discovery. But astronomers won't be surprised if the first message that is received takes many years to understand fully.

▼ *The Allen Telescope Array is being built north of San Francisco.*

# Unsolved Mysteries

Astronomers have already learned much about the universe. But science is also about the frontiers of knowledge—the things we don't know or understand yet. Many mysteries about the universe still remain. But since the pace of learning in astronomy is getting faster, it's possible that some of the questions on these pages will be answered by the time you are an adult.

## Could there have been life on another planet or moon in our solar system?

When we look at the planets and moons that orbit our Sun, there isn't one place besides the Earth where humans could survive. The other places are too hot or too cold. There is either no air, or the air would be poisonous to us. Four of the planets don't even have a solid surface. We know that life on Earth can be found on land and underwater and even in places where it is superhot and supercold. Are there places on other worlds where life might survive? Mars was warmer and wetter long ago, and maybe some life forms remain deep underground or are frozen in the planet's ice. Jupiter's moons Europa and Ganymede may have oceans of water under their crusts of ice. One day, scientists may send probes to dig beneath the ice crusts and explore the oceans for signs of life.

### WHAT DO WE WANT TO KNOW?

- Is the universe infinite or does it have some kind of limit?
- Will the universe ever die?
- What's it like inside a black hole?
- Will a big asteroid hit the Earth one day?
- Are there alien kids on another planet reading an astronomy book like this one right now?

Standing stones on Mars, each about one inch tall, may be connected with water that flowed in the past.

## Why is Titan the only moon with a thick atmosphere?

Although Saturn's moon Titan it is not the largest moon in our solar system, it is Saturn's largest moon and it is the only one to have a thick atmosphere. Scientists would like to know why. In fact, astronomers consider Titan to be one of the most interesting places in the solar system. Scientists wonder if there could be giant moons with atmospheres that have life on them? One day, they hope to know.

## Are there planets among the stars where humans could live?

Astronomers don't yet know if some of the planets around other stars might be more like Earth. NASA is planning to send a new mission into Earth's orbit, called *Kepler*, which may find planets the size of Earth among the stars. Whether such planets will have the kind of temperature or air that humans need to survive remains to be seen.

## How big and how small can a star get?

If a star-forming cloud is too big, it will split and form more than one star. If it's too small, it won't get hot enough to make energy in its core. It will become a failed star, something called a **brown dwarf**. But no one knows exactly where the limits are. Scientists once thought that stars couldn't get much bigger than the mass of a hundred Suns. But the Hubble Space Telescope has found some bigger stars.

◀ *Nicknamed the Pistol Star, the bright point in the middle of this picture is one of the biggest stars ever found. It shines with the light of ten million Suns.*

SOME SAY IT'S A MYSTERY THAT BUZZ AND I ARE FRIENDS, BUT IT'S A BIG ENOUGH GALAXY FOR THE BOTH OF US!

## What kind of stuff makes up most of the universe?

The universe reminds astronomers of an iceberg. The part of an iceberg that's easy to see is the tip that sticks out of the water. But a much larger part of the iceberg is underwater and far more difficult to see. In the same way, the visible part of our universe—the stars, the planets, the galaxies—may only be a small part of what's out there. Astronomers are finding all kinds of evidence for hidden stuff and strange energies in deep space. No one knows yet what this "dark matter" and "dark energy" are made of or how much of it there is, but already it's clear that there is more to our universe than meets the eye.

▼ *The future Terrestrial Planet Finder mission would search for planets like Earth around other stars.*

# Astronomy All-Stars

**Hipparchus (190–120 B.C.)** Greatest ancient Greek astronomer and a mathematician. Measured precession, the slow wobble of Earth's axis, the distance to the Moon, and the length of the year. Made the first star catalog.

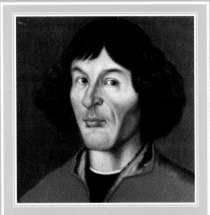

**Nicolaus Copernicus (1473–1543)** Polish doctor and astronomer. Suggested that the Sun, not Earth, is the center of the solar system.

**Galileo Galilei (1564–1642)** Italian mathematician and physicist. First to use a telescope to regularly observe the skies. Discovered Jupiter's moons, proved that Venus orbits the Sun, and showed that the Milky Way is made of stars.

**Johannes Kepler (1571–1630)** German astronomer and mathematician. Figured out the rules by which the planets move in their orbits. (Also wrote the first science-fiction story.)

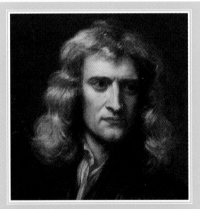

**Sir Isaac Newton (1642–1727)** English physicist. Considered by some people the greatest scientist of all time. Figured out the rules of motion and gravity. Designed the first reflecting (mirror) telescope.

**Edmund Halley (1656–1742).** English astronomer. Charted the course of many comets, including the returning one called Halley's Comet. Showed that stars slowly move across the sky over the centuries.

Every field of study has its heroes and legends. They are people who push the boundaries of understanding, challenge accepted beliefs, experiment, invent, and relentlessly pursue knowledge. These are some of astronomy's most famous innovators.

**Sir William Herschel (1738–1822)** German-English amateur astronomer. Discovered the planet Uranus and infrared radiation. Measured the Sun's motion through space and estimated the shape of the Milky Way.

**Henrietta Swan Leavitt (1868–1921)** American astronomer. Discovered characteristics of variable stars (called Cepheids) that allowed them to be used to measure distances to stars and galaxies.

**Edwin Hubble (1889–1953)** American astronomer. First to show that galaxies are separate islands of stars. Discovered the expansion of the universe and named the different types of galaxies.

**Cecilia Payne-Gaposchkin (1900–1979)** British-American astronomer. First showed that the stars were made mostly of the lightest element, hydrogen.

**Subrahmanyan Chandrasekhar (1910–1995)** Indian-American physicist. Explained the different ways that stars die and contributed to our understanding of black holes. He won the Nobel Prize in 1983.

**Frank Drake (1930–)** American astronomer. Founded the field of SETI (Search for Extraterrestrial Intelligence) and did the first search for radio signals from alien civilizations around other stars, in 1960.

# Everyday Astronomy

▲ Comet Hale-Bopp

▲ Partial lunar eclipse ▲ Partial solar eclipse ▲ Shooting star ▲ Aurora, as seen in Antarctica

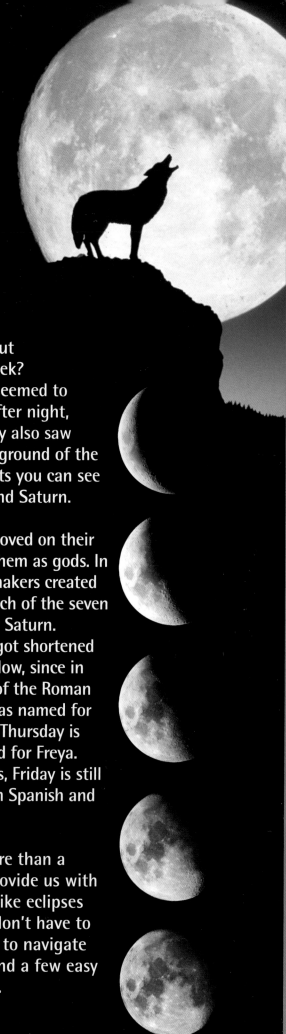

So much of our sense of time comes from changes in the sky. The rhythm of day and night is determined by the spinning of our planet on its axis. This day-and-night pattern helps us—and all living things—know when to rest and when to be active. The cycle of seasons is determined by the orbit of our tilted planet around the Sun. The seasons determine activities, such as planting and harvesting crops.

Days and nights based on Earth's rotation, months based on the cycle of the moon, and years based on our orbit around the Sun are natural time markers. But did you ever wonder why we have seven days in a week? Ancient astronomers saw that everything in the sky seemed to move around us once a day, as Earth turned. Night after night, the stars moved around the sky in the same way. They also saw seven objects in the sky that moved against the background of the stars. They are the Sun, the Moon, and the five planets you can see without a telescope: Mercury, Venus, Mars, Jupiter, and Saturn.

Ancient people thought that the seven objects that moved on their own must be very special. Some cultures thought of them as gods. In honor of these seven powerful sky objects, calendar makers created a unit of time that they called a week. They named each of the seven days after one of these objects. Saturday is named for Saturn. Sunday, of course, was named for the Sun. Moonday got shortened to Monday. The other four days are a bit harder to follow, since in English, the names of Viking gods were used instead of the Roman names usually associated with the planets. Tuesday was named for Tiw and Wednesday for Woden. Thursday is Thor's day and Friday was named for Freya. But in some European languages, Friday is still Venus's day: it's called *viernes* in Spanish and *vendredi* in French.

The sky, of course, provides more than a calendar. Cosmic events also provide us with incredible light shows—things like eclipses and meteor showers. And you don't have to be an astronomer to learn how to navigate the sky. All you have to do is find a few easy star patterns to be your guides.

▲ *Telescope*

# Marking Time

Our planet takes 24 hours to spin around once, and we call that a day. We imagine Earth turning on an axis—an imaginary stick running right through the middle of the planet. When the part of the world that you live in is facing the Sun, it's daytime. When Earth turns so your part of the world is facing away from the Sun, it's night. A year is the time it takes for a planet to go around the Sun once. Each Earth year consists of about 365¹/₄ days.

▲ When seen from space, day fades gradually into night on planet Earth.

## When do we have a one-quarter day in a year?

Instead of adding about a quarter day every year, we add a full day every four years, except in most years that end in zero. That fourth year is called a **leap year**. A leap year has 29 days in the month of February instead of the usual 28. A year is a leap year if it is divisible by four, but not if it is divisible by 100, unless it is also divisible by 400. By adding leap years, we keep the calendar in line with the actual movement of Earth around the Sun.

*I CAN GO AROUND THE SUN QUICKER THAN THE EARTH CAN!*

▼ Our solar system was born from a swirling cloud.

## FAST FACTS:

- The planet with the shortest year is Mercury. A year only lasts 88 Earth days there. The world with the longest year is the newly discovered dwarf planet beyond Pluto called Eris, which takes 560 Earth years to go around the Sun.

- During December, it is winter in the Northern Hemisphere of Earth. The days are short, and the nights are long. But the seasons are the opposite in the Southern Hemisphere. In December, Australia experiences the long days and short nights of summer.

- The Moon's orbit is expanding away from the Earth. It is getting farther away by about 1½ inches (4 cm) per year.

- A person born on February 29, 2004, will celebrate only 9 birthdays by 2040!

# Does the length of our day ever change?

It is changing—but very, very gradually. As the Moon's gravity rubs on our planet, the rate at which Earth spins slows down. The effect is very small. The day gets longer by one second every 50,000 years. Over millions of years, these changes will add up. In the distant past, our day was shorter by several hours, and in the far future, Earth will have days that are many hours longer.

Earth as seen from the Moon. The part of our planet that faces the Sun has day, the other half has night.

## Are days really longer during the summer and shorter in winter?

No matter what the season, the day is 24 hours long. But during the summer, the Sun's light is visible for more hours. On or about June 21, the first day of summer in the Northern Hemisphere, the Sun rises early and sets late, giving us the "longest day" of the year. For example, in the United States, there are on average 15 hours of daylight, and only 9 hours of darkness. On or about December 22, the "shortest day" of the year and the first day of winter in the Northern Hemisphere, the Sun rises later and sets earlier, leaving people in the United States in the dark for about 15 hours.

## Do all planets have night and day?

Yes. All the planets in our solar system spin around their axes, giving every planet a day-and-night pattern. But the length of the day/night pattern is not the same on all planets. Jupiter, which takes less than ten hours to turn, has the shortest day. Venus, which takes 243 Earth days to turn once on its axis, has the longest. Mars, like Earth, takes about 24 hours to complete its day-and-night cycle. Scientists think all the planets are spinning because the "mother cloud" that gave birth to our solar system was spinning as the planets formed within it.

# Seasons

Other than day and night, the most important cosmic rhythm in our lives is the changing of the seasons. The warmth of summer, the cold or rain of winter—these conditions can determine our survival and change the types of activities we can do. The number of hours of daylight also changes over the year, with more daylight in summer and longer nights during the winter.

▲ Winter

▲ Summer

## FAST FACTS:

- Although June 21 is the longest day of the year in the Northern Hemisphere, it is not the hottest. It's usually hotter in August. That's because it takes a while for the ground, the air, and the water on Earth to heat up. In the same way, a swimming pool is hottest in the late afternoon.

- At Earth's equator, the day and the night are both 12 hours long all year. People who live near the equator usually connect seasons with the amount of rain and not the amount of sunlight.

- The longest day of the year is called the summer solstice, and the shortest day, the winter solstice. Many cultures have a celebration at the winter solstice. The winter solstice marks a turning point when the Sun stops setting lower in the sky and begins to get higher in the sky each day. Now that's a reason to celebrate!

## During what season is Earth closest to the Sun?

When it's summer in the Northern Hemisphere, it's winter in the Southern Hemisphere. So, the season when Earth is closest to the Sun depends on where you live. For those who live above the equator in the Northern Hemisphere, in the United States or Canada, for example, Earth is closest to the Sun in the winter. In the Southern Hemisphere, in places such as Australia and Chile, Earth is closer to the Sun in the summer.

## How can it be winter when Earth is closest to the Sun?

It would seem to make sense that hot and cold seasons should be connected to how far our planet is from the Sun. But distance does not play a significant role in Earth's seasons. The main reason we have summer and winter is that Earth is *tilted*. Our axis doesn't run straight up and down but leans over a bit. This means that the top half of the world sometimes leans toward the Sun and sometimes leans away from the Sun. Earth's leaning is why the Sun seems higher in the sky during the summer and why there is more daylight in summer than in winter.

Like Earth, Saturn has a tilted axis and seasons, but they are much longer.

## Do other planets have seasons?

Whether a planet has seasons depends on whether it is leaning or not. Mercury and Jupiter are not leaning, so they don't have seasons the way Earth does. Mars and Saturn lean roughly the way the Earth does, so they do have seasons. But because Mars takes twice as long to go around the Sun, seasons on Mars are twice as long as on Earth. Uranus has very weird seasons because it orbits on its side, with its axis pointing toward the Sun or away from it.

## Why does the Sun's position in the sky cause seasons to be warmer or colder?

Try this little experiment in a dark room: shine a flashlight beam directly onto a wall. Can you see the bright spot where the flashlight is shining on the wall? Now make the flashlight lean by bending your wrist upward. See how the spot spreads out and isn't as bright anymore? In the summer, when our part of the planet leans into the Sun, its light comes in straighter and really heats every spot it reaches. In winter, the sunlight is much more spread out, and its heating ability is lessened. And because Earth is tilted away from the Sun during the winter, the Sun's light doesn't reach it for as long each day. That's why it's colder in winter.

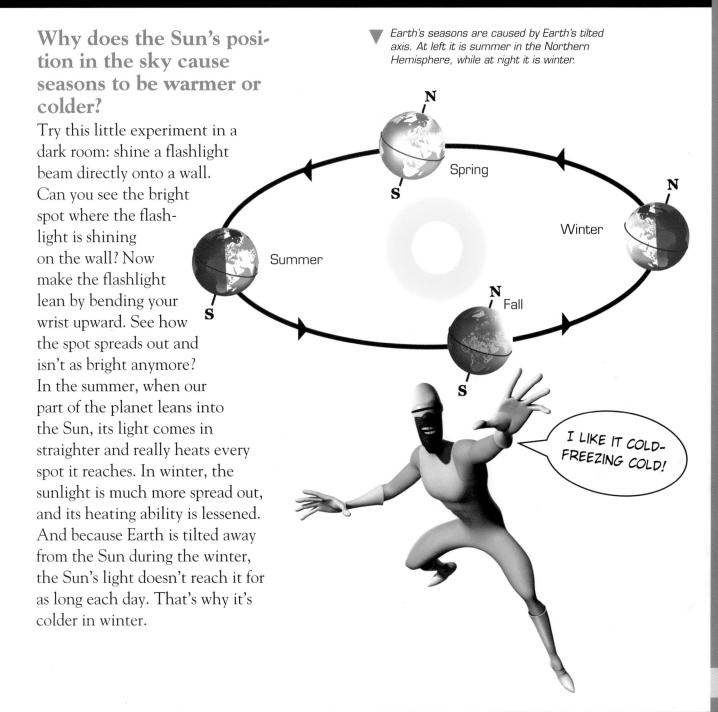

Earth's seasons are caused by Earth's tilted axis. At left it is summer in the Northern Hemisphere, while at right it is winter.

N
Spring
S

N
Winter

Summer

N
Fall
S

S

I LIKE IT COLD— FREEZING COLD!

# Phases of the Moon

If you look at the Moon in the sky over several weeks, you will notice that it looks different as time goes on. Sometimes the Moon appears round and bright, but at other times only a small crescent of it reflects light, while most of it is dark. The different amounts of light we see from the Moon are called its **phases**. Long ago, people discovered that the Moon's phases repeat in a regular cycle of about 29 days.

## Why does the Moon seem to change shape?

Moonlight is reflected sunlight. As the Moon goes around Earth, different parts of the Moon receive and reflect the light of the Sun. Half the Moon is always bright, and half is always dark. What the Moon looks like from Earth on any night depends on how much of the shiny side of the Moon is facing us.

Sunlight on the Moon shines at the same spot for 15 days. Here you can see one of the Apollo 17 astronauts and his Lunar Roving Vehicle in sunlight.

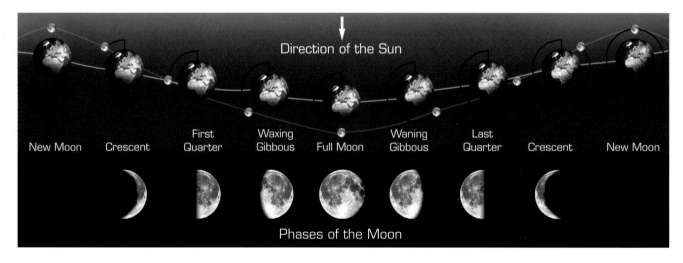

Direction of the Sun

| New Moon | Crescent | First Quarter | Waxing Gibbous | Full Moon | Waning Gibbous | Last Quarter | Crescent | New Moon |

Phases of the Moon

The top drawings show where the Moon and Earth are during each phase, while the bottom illustrations show what the Moon looks like from Earth during each phase.

### FAST FACT:

Because of the way the Moon rotates and orbits Earth, the same side of the Moon always faces us. Astronomers had to send a spacecraft to the other side of the Moon to learn what it was like. The first pictures of the other side were taken in 1959 by the Luna 3 spacecraft.

## Is there a dark side of the Moon?

As the Moon goes around Earth, all parts of it eventually get sunlight. But the Moon doesn't have 24-hour periods of day and night. If you stood on the surface of the Moon, you would see daylight for about 15 Earth days and the darkness of nighttime for another 15 Earth days.

## What are the different phases of the Moon?

When the Moon is in the same direction from Earth as the Sun, we cannot see it because the Sun is shining on the back side of the Moon. The side that's facing us doesn't show because it needs the reflection of the Sun to be seen. We call this phase of the Moon the "new moon." As the Moon goes around Earth, we soon see a little crescent of light reflecting off it. When the Moon has gone one quarter of the way around us, during the phase we call the first quarter, we see the Moon half lit up and half dark. The Moon continues to orbit Earth, until it is on the other side of Earth, away from the Sun. Then the Sun shines on the whole side of the Moon that we see. This phase is called the "full moon." As the Moon continues around, less and less of it has sunlight on it. At the third-quarter phase, we see the Moon half bright and half dark again. Then we just see a crescent that gets smaller with each passing night. And then, 29½ days after the cycle began, we are back to the new moon.

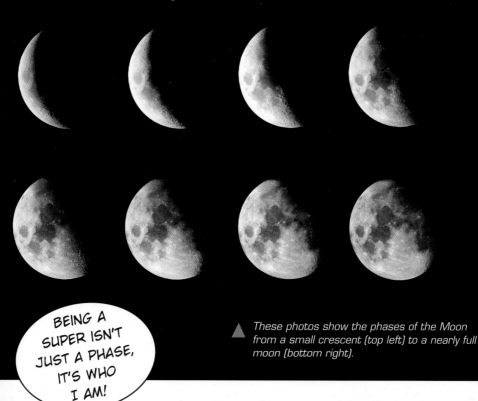

These photos show the phases of the Moon from a small crescent (top left) to a nearly full moon (bottom right).

> BEING A SUPER ISN'T JUST A PHASE, IT'S WHO I AM!

## Why does the Moon look bigger when it's close to the horizon than when it's up in the sky?

When the full moon is close to the horizon, it appears to have grown in size. This is called the **moon illusion**.

The Moon does not actually grow or shrink as it moves through the sky. It's the way humans see it that changes. When we see the Moon behind houses, trees, or cars, it looks huge in comparison to those objects. When we see the Moon alone in the middle of the dark sky, we have nothing to compare it to, so it appears smaller.

# Moon Madness & Lore

The Moon is the cosmic object that's closest to us and easiest to see in the night sky. Over thousands of years, humans have created more stories, legends, and questions about the Moon than about any other astronomical object. The questions that follow here show just some of the lore people believe about the Moon. And the scientific explanations provided will help you to better understand the night sky.

## Is there a face in the Moon?

When we see sunlight reflecting from the Moon, some parts of the Moon are darker and some are lighter. The darker areas are made up of round spots, formed when large rocks hit the Moon's surface long ago. Dark lava from inside the Moon spilled into the round craters. People in many cultures thought they could see a pattern in the light and dark spots on the Moon. Many saw a face and made up stories about "the man in the Moon." Others saw a fox or a toad. Take a look at the full moon sometime, and you can make up your own story of what the Moon's pattern resembles.

### FAST FACT:

What do you see when you gaze upon a full moon? Some people see a boy and a girl carrying a bucket of water in the dark areas of the Moon. They would be upside down in the picture to the right. This may be where the nursery rhyme about Jack and Jill comes from. (The story is actually Scandinavian, where the boy's name is related to the word for "increase" and the girl's name to the word for "dissolve." And that's what the Moon does each month—increase and dissolve.)

## Do people really act strangely during a full moon?

The idea that the full moon makes people act crazy is an old folktale which is still repeated today. The word *lunatic*, which means "person who behaves in an odd or crazy way," comes from the Latin word for moon, which is *luna*. But scientists have looked at police and hospital records to see if more crazy, violent things really happen during the full moon than during the other phases. The answer is *no*. Apparently, people can act strangely during *all* the phases of the Moon. Perhaps we are just more likely to notice crazy things when the full moon's light brightens the night.

▼ The dark areas on the Moon are giant round craters filled with lava.

## Can the position of the Moon at the moment we are born affect our lives?

There is a big difference between astronomy—the scientific study of the universe—and astrology—the ancient belief that the Sun, Moon, and planets influence our lives. Scientists have run experiments about astrology, as they do about everything. None of these tests have been able to show that astrology works. And there is no reason why the location of the Sun, Moon, and planets at the time you were born should have any effect on what kind of person you will turn out to be. Objects in space are much too far away to determine the direction of our lives.

▲ Myths and folklore have inspired moviemakers to create many scary movies with spooky scenes featuring the full moon.

WHEN I'M FEELING BLUE, I DON'T SHOW UP TWICE— I DISAPPEAR!

## What's a "blue moon"?

Believe it or not, the phrase "blue moon" has nothing to do with the color of the Moon. Since the cycle of the Moon's phases is 29½ days and a month can be 30 or 31 days, sometimes two full moons can occur in the same month. Astronomers call the second full moon in that month a **blue moon**. Blue moons don't happen on a regular schedule, but the average time between them is about three years. When people say that something happens "once in a blue moon," they mean it happens infrequently.

## Do wolves howl at the full moon?

Wolves are primarily nocturnal animals, which means they do much of their roaming and hunting at night. They howl as a means of communicating with their pack mates, and they do it just as often under a new moon as under a full moon.

# Eclipses of the Sun & Moon

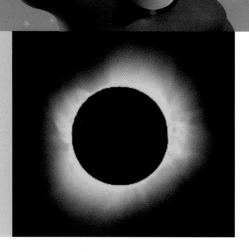

Imagine this: in the middle of the day, the sky turns black. Animals run around in confusion, not knowing whether it's time to sleep or to be awake. Then, after a few scary minutes, the Sun begins to emerge from the dark disk that covered it. Soon, the light returns. To ancient people, such a spectacle was terrifying. But today we know that these rare events are perfectly natural. Astronomers call them total **solar eclipses**. The Moon has eclipses, too.

## What causes an eclipse of the Sun?

It's a neat coincidence. The Sun, as seen from Earth, seems to take up exactly the same amount of room in the sky as the Moon. Sure, the Sun is a lot bigger, but it's also farther away, which makes it seem small. Usually, the orbits of the Sun and Moon are not lined up. But every so often, from our line of sight, their orbits cross. Then it's possible for the Moon to pass in front of the Sun. When the Moon completely covers the Sun, we call it a **total eclipse**; when only a part of the Sun is covered, it's a **partial eclipse**. A total solar eclipse lasts no more than a few minutes. But when you can see the dark Sun's faint atmosphere flickering and glowing from behind the Moon, it's a really awesome sight.

▲ When the Sun is covered by the Moon, you can see the Sun's faint outer layers glowing.

## Where do I go to see a total eclipse?

Total eclipses of the Sun are only visible in a small region, just 100 miles (160 km) or so wide. Eclipses can happen anywhere on Earth, and you have to be in the path of totality to see the full effect. People who are eclipse fans travel all around the world just for the 1 to 3 minutes when the Moon covers the Sun.

▼ In a total eclipse of the Sun, the Sun, Moon, and Earth are all lined up. The Moon's shadow falls on a small part of Earth.

### FAST FACTS:

An eclipse occurs once or twice a year somewhere around the world. However, the average spot on Earth sees an eclipse of the Sun only once every 410 years. That's because each eclipse is only visible over a small part of our planet. For example, the next total eclipse visible in the United States will occur in 2017.

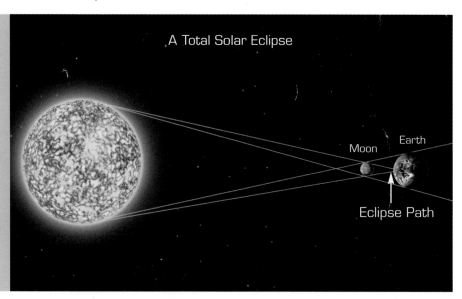

A Total Solar Eclipse

Moon    Earth

Eclipse Path

## Is a solar eclipse dangerous?

Before people understood that eclipses were natural events, they used to think that the sudden disappearance of the Sun would bring on disaster. Today, we know that's not true. But there is one danger that eclipse watchers do have to worry about: looking at the Sun can really damage your eyes. When the Sun is not eclipsed, looking at the Sun is so painful that few people are tempted to do it. During an eclipse, however, when the Sun is partly covered and everyone is fascinated, it's easy to be drawn into looking at it. But looking at even a partly covered Sun is still quite dangerous.

▲ A total solar eclipse

THE INCREDIBLES ALWAYS ECLIPSE EVIL!

▲ Earth's shadow falls across the full Moon during a lunar eclipse.

## What causes eclipses of the Moon?

Shadows happen when solid bodies block sunlight. Earth also casts a shadow into space, opposite the Sun. Space is black, just like the shadow, so most of the time we can't see Earth's shadow. But if the Moon is just opposite the Sun, then Earth's shadow can fall on it. The Sun, Earth, and Moon have to be lined up just right, but when they are, Earth's shadow falls right on the Moon. Then we see a **lunar eclipse**. The Moon is full at these times, and it looks quite dramatic as it slowly goes dark. Lunar eclipses occur once or twice a year. They last longer than eclipses of the Sun and can be seen from everywhere on Earth that the Moon is visible. And they're also perfectly safe to view.

# Shooting Stars & Meteor Showers

If you watch the sky on a dark night, you may see a shooting star—a brief, bright streak of light crossing the sky. Some people call these flashes of light "falling stars," but they have nothing at all to do with stars. They are small pieces of dirt or rock that hit Earth's layers of air traveling so fast that they burn up. Astronomers call them **meteors**.

## How big are meteors?

Typical meteors are about the size of a pea. If bigger chunks hit Earth's atmosphere, they glow much more brightly, producing something called a fireball. Fireballs burn longer and can even be visible during the daytime.

## Do meteors ever land on Earth?

Yes! If a piece as big as a bowling ball—or bigger—enters our atmosphere, it may not burn up completely. When such chunks make it down to the ground, astronomers call them **meteorites**. It is believed that a giant meteorite hitting Earth's surface led to the extinction of the dinosaurs. Its explosion caused worldwide fires and later, huge clouds of dust, smoke, and dirt to cover the planet, blocking the Sun. As a result, many of Earth's plants and animals became extinct.

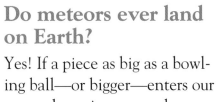

◄ *A brilliant fireball burns up in our atmosphere above Norway in 1999.*

## FAST FACT:

Astronomers estimate that about 100 tons (200,000 pounds) of cosmic dirt hits our planet's atmosphere *each day*! Almost all of it burns up high above us before reaching Earth's surface.

## Can we see meteorites that have landed on Earth?

Many are on display in science and nature museums. If you want to find one on your own, head to Antarctica. It's not that more meteorites fall there than in other place, but because the ground there is pure white ice all year long, any rock you'd find would be easy to spot and would most likely have come from space!

## How fast do meteors hit our atmosphere?

Typical meteors enter at anywhere from 22,000 to 88,000 miles per hour (36,000 to 142,000 km/h). Their temperatures reach thousands of degrees as they burn up. They are so hot that we can see the glow even though they are 30 to 60 miles (49 to 97 km) up in the sky when they disappear.

WATCH ME WIN THE FIVE-METEOR RACE!

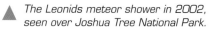

The Leonids meteor shower in 2002, seen over Joshua Tree National Park.

## Why can you see a lot of shooting stars on certain nights?

Big chunks of ice and dirt that come from deep space are called comets. Sometimes they come close to the Sun. When a comet's ice is heated, it turns to gas, leaving dust behind. Some comets swing by the Sun again and again over the years, leaving behind a trail of dirt. When Earth in its yearly orbit enters this stream of dirt, we can see many meteors on the same night. These events are called **meteor showers**, and the days we see them can be predicted. The chart on page 117 shows you some of the best-known meteor showers, which comets they come from, and when to look for them in the Northern Hemisphere.

Comet Hale-Bopp

# Auroras & Other Lights

When people shoot fireworks into the sky, it can make for a beautiful sight. But nature sets up its own fireworks sometimes, and they can be every bit as exciting as the ones humans make. Near the north and south poles, people who look up at the sky can sometimes see a huge, colorful curtain of light called an **aurora**. Other names for auroras are the northern lights and southern lights.

## What causes an aurora?

The lights of the aurora are actually caused by the Sun. It's not the Sun's *light* that does it but the Sun's *wind*. Every day, the Sun releases a huge number of tiny particles, which blow toward the planets at speeds of a million miles per hour (1.6 million km/h). Because they move so fast, the particles of the Sun's wind have a lot of energy. When they hit Earth's atmosphere, they cause the air to glow in a shimmering display.

> AURORAS ARE PRETTY COLORFUL, BUT I PREFER A VIOLET FORCE FIELD!

▲ *An aurora above the Earth as seen by the astronauts aboard the International Space Station*

## Why can't you see an aurora everywhere on Earth?

Our planet acts as a giant magnet, with north and south magnetic poles close to where Earth's north and south poles are. The magnet actually keeps the particles of the Sun's wind away from Earth everywhere except at the poles. There the particles can come down and get the air charged and glowing. This is why you see auroras at locations that are far north (such as Alaska) and never near Earth's equator.

## FAST FACT:

**Storms on the Sun**

Sometimes the Sun has a "storm," which is an unusually strong wind of particles. Then, the particles can damage our orbiting satellites, disturb cell phone service, and even cause power blackouts. A sun storm in 1989 knocked out power to the city of Montreal, in Canada, for nine hours. During such storms, auroras can be especially intense.

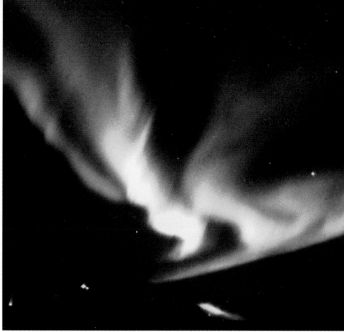

▲ The blue ring at Saturn's south pole in this photo is an aurora.

▲ Auroras look like great curtains of light in the sky.

## Can there be auroras on other planets, too?

Any planet that acts like a magnet can have aurora displays near its north and south magnetic poles. Space probes that have gone by Jupiter and Saturn, for example, have recorded huge auroras on these giant planets.

## What causes the ring around the Moon?

Sometimes, especially on cold nights, you can see a beautiful ring of light around the Moon. Such rings are caused by ice crystals three to six miles up in our atmosphere. Like little diamonds, the ice crystals bend the light of the Moon from every direction and send it back to us. The result is a beautiful circle of light around the Moon.

▼ The red colors of sunset

## What else causes lights in the sky?

A ring around the Sun sometimes occurs when there are ice crystals in the clouds high above our heads. When there are drops of water in the atmosphere—for example, right after it rains—the water droplets can split the colors of sunlight into a rainbow. And if there is a lot of dust and dirt in our atmosphere, the setting sun can make the evening sky glow with reddish colors.

# Finding the Constellations

Finding your way around the sky is like getting to know a new town or city. At first, you feel lost. But then, slowly, you get to know the different landmarks and feel more comfortable. In the sky, too, there are guideposts such as the Big Dipper that can help you find your way around the stars. The answers on these pages will help you find constellations in Earth's Northern Hemisphere. People in the Southern Hemisphere see different star patterns.

## How do I find the Big Dipper?

Depending on where you live, if you face north, you can usually find the seven bright stars that make up the Big Dipper. They can be seen every night of the year—higher in the sky in spring, lower in fall. The Dipper looks like a giant square spoon, or ladle, with a long handle.

## What can I find using the Big Dipper as a guide?

The two stars of the bowl of the Dipper opposite the handle are called the "pointer stars." They point to Polaris, the north star. Polaris was called the "thumbtack of the sky" because it doesn't appear to turn—all the other stars appear to turn around it. If you keep looking in the direction that the pointer stars point toward, you will see a W-shaped group of stars. This star pattern, or constellation, is called Cassiopeia.

SOON, THE WHOLE WORLD WILL TURN AROUND ME!

## Where is Orion the Hunter?

Orion is visible in the winter and spring. You can usually spot it because the hunter has a belt of three bright stars that make a short straight line in the sky. Look for it toward the south, moving from southeast to southwest between November and April. Two bright stars are easily visible above and below the belt. The one above is Betelgeuse (Orion's shoulder). The one below is called Rigel (Orion's knee).

### FAST FACT:

The stars are millions or billions of years old. So the stars and constellations you see are the same ones that all humans have seen since they first lived in small tribes on the African plains. Imagine what Caesar, Moses, the great emperors of China, and all the leaders of history thought when they saw the very same stars that you see tonight.

▼ The Big Dipper can serve as a guide to other harder to spot stars and constellations.

## What other stars can I find with Orion as my guide?

If you face south on a winter evening and follow the belt of Orion right to left (toward the east), you will come to the brightest star in the nighttime sky. It is called Sirius, and it is one of the closest stars to our Sun. Sirius also looks bright because the star shines 24 times brighter than the Sun. Sirius is part of the constellation called Canis Major, which means "Big Dog" in Latin. Follow the belt of Orion the other way, from left to right, and you will come to a bright star called Aldebaran. This red star is the "bloodshot eye" of the constellation Taurus, the bull.

## Why can't we see stars during the day?

The stars are always there during the day, but the Sun's light is too bright for us to be able to see them. Every once in a while, something in the sky does become bright enough for us to see through the sunlight. You can often see the Moon during the day and the planet Venus when it's bright. And in the very rare case when a star explodes, its light may be visible in the daytime for several weeks.

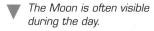
*The Moon is often visible during the day.*

*Orion is one of the most recognizable constellations in the winter sky.*

# A Sky Watcher's Calendar

Any clear night is a perfect time for watching the sky. In addition to the Moon, there is usually at least one planet visible. The dates of meteor showers are predictable each year, although some years there are more shooting stars than others. And every once in a while, there are some special sky events that you might enjoy watching out for. Many sky watchers keep a journal of what they have seen and when.

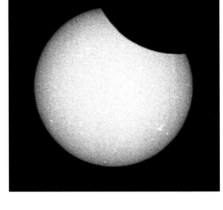

▲ A total solar eclipse can take more than an hour to become complete.

## When will there be a month with a blue moon?

A blue moon is the second full moon in a month with two full moons. The next ones will be:
- December 2009: full moon on December 2 and December 31
- August 2012: full moons on August 1 and August 31
- July 2015: full moons on July 1 and July 31

## When will an eclipse of the Sun be visible in North America?

The next total solar eclipse visible from the United States and Canada will be August 21, 2017, so you have time to get ready. But there will be a partial eclipse, in which the Sun will appear as a ring around the Moon, on May 20, 2012. It will be visible only from the western part of North America.

## When will an eclipse of the Moon be visible in North America?

- August 28, 2007: total eclipse of the Moon in the morning before the Sun rises. Visible throughout the United States and Canada.
- February 20, 2008: total eclipse of the Moon around midnight. Visible throughout the United States and Canada.
- December 20, 2010: total eclipse of the Moon in the late evening. Visible throughout the United States and Canada.
- April 14, 2014: total eclipse of the Moon in the late evening. Visible throughout the United States and Canada.

DAHLING, I CAN MAKE YOU A FABULOUS RAINCOAT FOR THESE SHOWERS. I INSIST!

## FAST FACTS:

### Upcoming Sky Events
- Dec. 23, 2007: the Moon and Mars will be next to each other in the sky in the early evening.
- July 2008 to June 2009: the rings of Saturn will be seen edgewise from Earth, and the rings will seem to disappear.
- Feb. 21, 2015: Venus and Mars will be next to each other in the sky in the early evening.

## When can I see a meteor shower?

This chart lists some of the best regularly occurring meteor showers.

**METEOR SHOWERS**

| Name of Shower | Date of Best Viewing | Comet It Comes From | Number of Meteors Visible Per Hour |
|---|---|---|---|
| Quadrantids | January 3 | 2003 EH1 (comet remnant) | 30–90 |
| Lyrids | April 22 | Comet Thatcher | 10–20 |
| Perseids | August 12 | Comet Swift-Tuttle | 40–100 |
| Orionids | October 20 | Comet Halley | 15–20 |
| Leonids | November 17 | Comet Tempel-Tuttle | 10–100 |
| Geminids | December 14 | Phaethon (comet remnant) | 40–90 |

NOTE: Some of the comets have come around so often that they have lost most of their ice. If they are made mostly of dirt, they are called comet remnants in the chart, rather than comets.

▲ This is a map showing what the world looks like from space at night. You can see the lights of major cities.

## Light Pollution: Losing the Dark

In the past, most people had a much clearer view of the night sky. But artificial light from homes, workplaces, and street-lights has made objects in the sky less visible. Astronomers call this **light pollution**. Because of light pollution, telescopes must be moved to locations very far from civilization to see the faintest stars and galaxies. Scientists and planners are working to reduce light pollution by placing shields around street lamps to direct the light down and by finding more efficient lights to install around cities.

# Family Astronomy Activities

## Choosing Equipment

There are different kinds of telescopes and binoculars for different purposes and budgets. Before buying any tools, see if you can "take a test drive" by borrowing one from someone you know. Talk to other star-watching enthusiasts and ask for their advice, too. Remember: if where you live has a lot of lights, you'll want something portable that you can easily carry to a dark place. Have maps of the sky with you (such as those on pages 120 and 121 of this book) to help you know what to look for. Or get a star wheel (sometimes called a planisphere), which will help you pinpoint what's in the sky as seen from your location on Earth.

## Getting Started

The first step is to find a dark, safe place to observe the sky. Then you need to give your eyes 15 to 20 minutes to adapt to the dark. To find your way around and read your charts, bring a flashlight with a red bulb. In the dark, red light doesn't hurt your eyes the way white light does. You can make a red flashlight by taping some red cloth or plastic over the lighted end of a regular flashlight. And don't forget to dress warmly if you are going to be outside at night for a while. The first time you set out, just try to find easy things like the Moon; a bright planet, such as Venus; or an easy-to-spot star group, such as the Big Dipper. You don't need any special equipment to see these objects, just your eyes.

## Using Instruments

Once you've practiced with your eyes, you can move on to a pair of binoculars or a small telescope. Among the easiest things you can look at is the Moon, where you can see craters of all sizes caused by rocks that hit its surface long ago. You can also try to see the rings of Saturn or the four big moons around Jupiter. In the constellation of Orion, look for the sword hanging from his belt, which has a reddish fuzz in the middle of it. This is a place in which new stars are being born right now. Some Web sites to help you learn about the sky and know what to look for are recommended on page 122.

Reading about astronomy can be a lot of fun, but getting outside and observing the sky yourself is even better. It's amazing to think that by using almost any good binoculars or small telescope today, we can see more in the sky than Galileo ever could in his whole lifetime. If you don't have binoculars, perhaps a relative or friend, or your school, might have a pair you can borrow.

## Watching Meteor Showers

Meteor watching can be a fun activity for the whole family. On a night when a meteor shower is predicted (see page 117), find a safe place away from city lights with an open view of the sky. Now get comfortable! A reclining lawn chair is ideal, but an ordinary lawn chair will work just fine—or even a sleeping bag on the ground. Be sure to bring a jacket or a blanket to keep you warm and insect repellent to keep the bugs away. Now just settle back, allow your eyes to adjust to the darkness, and scan the sky with your eyes—no need for binoculars or telescopes. Be patient. Soon you will see a fast streak of light shooting across the sky—and then another, and another! You might even want to have a friendly competition with your fellow sky watchers to see who can spot the most meteors.

## Sharing the Sky

There are more than 500 amateur astronomy clubs in the United States and more around the world. Amateur astronomers are people who enjoy astronomy as a hobby. Many of the clubs hold "star parties"—special events at which members take their telescopes out to a park or other public place and invite everyone to look through them. There are also some Web sites to help you find an astronomy club near you listed on page 122. Participating in a star party is a great way to get to use different telescopes and binoculars before buying them.

### Some Astronomy Activities for Families

- Create a Sky Log, where family members can write about their observations. Include columns for date and time and leave plenty of space for everyone to describe what they saw.

- Help organize an Astronomy Day at your school or library.

- Cut out articles on the latest discoveries, and look for cool photos on nasa.gov, or hubblesite.org. Paste them into an astronomy scrapbook.

- Check out the family astronomy Web site, www.astrosociety.org/education/family.html

- Take a trip to a planetarium in your area.

# Star Maps

This map shows the sky during summer evenings.
Since the positions of the stars change over the
course of the summer, this map is best
used around 10 pm on June 1
or 8 pm on July 1.

The star maps on these pages show the constellations visible during summer and winter evenings in the United States. The names of the constellations are shown in capital letters; the names of bright stars are shown in lowercase letters. To use each map, hold it in front of you. Turn it until the direction you are facing is at the bottom. Use a compass to find north, or remember that the Sun sets roughly in the west.

This map shows the sky during winter evenings. It's best used around 10 pm on December 1 or 8 pm on January 1.

# Websites

**Great Pictures:**
- Hubble Space Telescope: http://hubblesite.org/gallery/
- NASA Planetary Photojournal:
  http://photojournal.jpl.nasa.gov
- Astronomy Picture of the Day:
  http://antwrp.gsfc.nasa.gov/apod/
- National Observatory Gallery:
  http://www.noao.edu/image_gallery/
- NASA's Picture Galleries:
  http://www.nasa.gov/multimedia/imagegallery/

**Finding an Astronomy Club Near You:**
- http://skytonight.com/community/organizations/
- http://astroleague.org/al/general/society.html

**Astronomy Web Sites for Kids:**
- Amazing Space from the Hubble Space Telescope:
  http://amazing-space.stci.edu/
- NASA's Star Child (for kids under 14):
  http://starchild.gsfc.nasa.gov/
- NASA's Imagine the Universe (for kids 14 and up):
  http://imagine.gsfc.nasa.gov/
- Windows to the Universe: http://www.windows.ucar.edu
- The Family Astronomy Project: http://astrosociety.org/
  education/family.html

**Organizations to Check Out:**
- NASA for kids:
  http://www.nasa.gov/audience/forkids/home/index.html
- The Astronomical Society of the Pacific:
  http://www.astrosociety.org
- The Planetary Society: http://www.planetary.org
- The SETI Institute (all about the search for life among the
  stars): http://www.seti.org

**Magazines on Astronomy:**
- *Astronomy* magazine: http://www.astronomy.com
- *Sky & Telescope* magazine: http://skytonight.com

# Conclusion

On this page you'll find some of the best Web sites for keeping up with astronomy. If you want to talk to others about what you are learning, many cities have astronomy clubs that welcome kids and families. If you are interested, ask your parents to help you check out one of these local clubs.

One of the most exciting things about astronomy is that many discoveries about the universe were not predicted by anyone until they happened. Scientists expect many more surprises in the years ahead. In the next decade, new spacecraft will land on Mars, orbit Venus, and fly by Pluto. New systems of planets may be discovered around other stars, some of them perhaps even stranger than the ones we know today. Who knows all the things that nature has up her sleeve. When it comes to the wonderful world of space—the sky's the limit!

# Glossary

**Amino acid** – The building blocks that make up the proteins in living things on Earth

**Asterism** – A group of stars in the sky that makes an interesting pattern (but is only part of a constellation); an example is the Big Dipper

**Asteroid** – A chunk of rock that is too small to be a planet and is in orbit around a star

**Asteroid belt** – A zone containing many asteroids (such as the one between Mars and Jupiter)

**Atmosphere** – The layer of air around a planet or moon (or the layer of thin, hot gas around a star)

**Atom** – The smallest piece of an element that still has all the properties of that element; for example, a gold atom is the smallest piece of gold there can be

**Aurora** – Curtains of colored light in the sky near the north and south magnetic poles of a planet

**Axis** – An imaginary line through the middle of a planet around which it spins

**Barred spiral galaxy** – A spiral galaxy with a bar of stars through its middle

**Big Bang** – The explosion that started the universe; all of space, time, matter, and energy begin with the Big Bang

**Black hole** – A dead star that has collapsed so much that nothing, not even light, can escape from it

**Black dwarf** – A dead star that was once a white dwarf but has cooled off

**Blue moon** – A second full moon in a month

**Brown dwarf** – A failed star; one that cannot get hot enough inside to make its own energy

**Carbon** – A type of atom made by stars that is the key element in life as we know it

**Cepheid** – A kind of star that gets a little bit brighter and dimmer on a regular schedule; Cepheids can be used to measure distances to stars

**Comet** – A chunk of dirty ice in orbit around a star

**Constellation** – One of 88 sections into which astronomers divide the whole sky around the Earth (another, older, meaning is: an interesting pattern of stars, such as Orion)

**Core** – The central part of a planet or a star; the core of a star is where fusion happens

**Crater** – A round hole in the surface of a planet or moon; it is made when a chunk of rock or ice from space hits the planet or moon and explodes

**Crust** – The outer layer of a solid planet

**Day** – The time it takes a planet to spin (rotate) once

**Dwarf planet** – A world that is round, but is too small to have a cleared orbit; Ceres was the first dwarf planet discovered in our solar system

**Earth satellite** – A machine (capsule with instruments) in orbit around the Earth

**Eclipse** – When the Moon gets in front of the Sun, or when the Earth gets between the Sun and the Moon; the first is called a solar eclipse, the second a lunar eclipse

**Electromagnetic radiation** – Waves given off by objects all around the universe; light is the best-known example

**Elliptical galaxy** – A galaxy with a balloon or blimp shape

**Equator** – An imaginary circle around the middle of a planet, halfway between its north and south poles

**Escape speed** – The speed you need to attain to get away from the gravity of a world

**Expanding universe** – The idea that all the galaxy clusters are moving away from all the other galaxy clusters (that space itself is stretching)

**Fusion** – The process that makes stars shine and hydrogen bombs explode; atoms come together under hot conditions and make energy

**Galaxy** – A giant group of millions or billions of stars

**Galaxy cluster** – A group of anywhere from dozens to thousands of galaxies, all "hanging out" together in space

**Gravity** – A force that pulls all objects in the universe toward all other objects; the gravity we know best is the gravity of the Earth, the force that pulls all of us toward the Earth and gives us our feeling of weight

**Greenhouse effect** – The warming of a planet by gases that let sunlight through but don't let heat escape

**Irregular galaxy** – A galaxy whose shape is not spiral or elliptical but looks more like a disorganized group of stars

**Kuiper belt** – The region of dwarf planets and icy chunks beyond the orbit of Neptune; Pluto was the first member of this belt to be discovered

**Leap year** – A year with 366 days in it; we have a leap year every four years (except most years ending with 00)

**Light pollution** – The presence of light on the night side of the Earth from houses, advertising signs, streetlights, and other sources, which interferes with observing objects in the sky

**Light year** – The distance that light travels in one year; equals about 6 trillion (million million) miles (or almost 10 trillion kilometers)

**Local Group** – The several dozen galaxies with which our Milky Way moves together through space

**Lunar eclipse** – When the Earth's shadow falls on the Moon; when the Earth gets between the Sun and the Moon

**Meteor** – A piece of dirt, rock, or ice from space that burns up high in the Earth's atmosphere, creating a flash of light; sometimes called a "shooting star"

**Meteor shower** – A time when many meteors can be seen; on these nights the Earth goes through old dust (dirt) left behind by a comet

# Glossary (Continued)

**Meteorite** – A chunk of rock that falls from space and survives its trip through the Earth's atmosphere

**Molecule** – A combination of atoms, bound together; for example, water is a molecule made up of hydrogen and oxygen atoms

**Moon** – A world made of rock or ice that orbits a planet

**Moon illusion** – The Moon looks bigger near the horizon than when it is high in the sky

**Nebula** – A cloud of gas and dust out among the stars; a nebula can surround just one star or can extend many light years

**Nucleus** – The center of an atom (made of protons and neutrons) or the center of a galaxy

**Observatory** – A place where there are one or more telescopes used for astronomy. Ancient observatories did not have telescopes, but were places used to study the sky.

**Oort Cloud** – A region far beyond the planets where there are billions of icy chunks; new comets can come inward from this "cloud"

**Orbit** – The path that one body in space takes when it goes around another body

**Parallax shift** – How much an object appears to change its position when seen from two different places; in astronomy, this is a way of measuring distances to nearer stars by looking at them from two different places in the Earth's orbit

**Partial eclipse** – An eclipse in which only part of the Sun is covered by the Moon or only part of the Moon is in Earth's shadow

**Phases of the Moon** – The different "shapes" of the Moon as seen from Earth; how much of the Moon we see lit up by sunlight during the month

**Planet** – A world (of fairly large size) that orbits a star; planets must be round and not orbit in a belt or zone of similar objects

**Planetary probe** – A spacecraft that flies by, orbits, or lands on another planet

**Prominence** – A giant eruption of hot gas from the Sun; often looks like a loop or arc

**Protostar** – A star that is just being born out of a cloud of gas and dust but has not yet started fusion

**Quasar** – A distant galaxy, whose center is so bright that it looks like a star when we see it from far away

**Radar** – A kind of radio wave that astronomers have bounced off planets, asteroids, and rings to find out more about these worlds.

**Radio array** – A group of radio telescopes used together to get more detailed information about things in space that give off radio waves

**Radio telescope** – A large metal dish used to gather and focus radio waves from space

**Radio waves** – A kind of electromagnetic radiation that has much longer waves than light; we use them for communication on Earth, and they also come to us from objects in space

**Red giant** – An old star that has swollen to a huge size; when our Sun becomes a red giant, it will be bigger than the whole orbit of Mars

**Reflector telescope** – A telescope that uses a mirror to collect light

**Refractor telescope** – A telescope that uses a lens to collect light

**Revolve** – To go completely around another object; for example, the Earth revolves around the Sun

**Rotate** – To spin on an axis (to turn)

**Shepherd moon** – A small moon near the edge of a ring around a planet; such moons keep the edges of rings from spreading out

**Solar eclipse** – An eclipse of the Sun; when the Moon covers up the Sun as seen from some part of the Earth

**Solar system** – The Sun and the family of planets, dwarf planets, moons, asteroids, and comets that go around it

**Spiral galaxy** – A galaxy that looks like a pinwheel—a flat disk with a little bulge in the middle and most of the stars in the disk arranged into spiral arms

**Star** – A giant ball of hot gas that shines under its own power

**Star Cluster** – A group of stars that are born together and "hang out" in space together; clusters can have dozens to millions of stars as members

**Starburst galaxy** – A galaxy that has recently collided with another one and has a lot of new stars forming as a result of the collision

**Sunspot** – a dark area on the Sun, which is a little cooler than the rest of it

**Supercluster of galaxies** – A group of galaxy clusters; the Milky Way is part of the Virgo Supercluster, for example

**Supernova** – A star that is exploding at the end of its life; such an explosion shines very brightly for a short while

**Telescope** – A device used by astronomers to collect light (or other waves) and show dimmer objects or more detail than our eyes alone can see

**Total eclipse** – An eclipse in which the Moon completely covers the Sun, or the Earth's shadow completely covers the Moon

**Universe** – Everything that we can know about (all of the objects and the space beyond the Earth)

**Void** – A region of space between superclusters where there are fewer galaxies

**White dwarf** – a shrunken dead star, which is white-hot from dying; when our Sun becomes a white dwarf, it will be only about twice the size of planet Earth

**Year** – The time it takes a planet to go around the Sun. Earth's year is about 365 days long

# Index

# Photo Credits